"What's going on?" Jude demanded with a frown of bewilderment, watching the baby cling to Tansy like a little limpet and dab playful kisses across Tansy's face in what was obviously a regular game between them.

In the ghastly silence that stretched inside the limousine, Tansy, having secured Posy in the car seat, broke out in nervous perspiration. "I'm really, *really* sorry that I didn't tell you about her beforehand," she whispered guiltily. "I was scared you would change your mind about marrying me."

Jude shot glittering dark golden eyes to her corner of the limousine and flung her a sardonic appraisal. "You think?"

"I'll grovel if you want me to but please don't shout in front of Posy. I don't want her to get upset," Tansy confided. "If you're *still* taking me to Greece with you—"

"You're my wife now. I don't see that I have much choice." Jude ground out that admission.

Lynne Graham was born in Northern Ireland and has been a keen romance reader since her teens. She is very happily married to an understanding husband who has learned to cook since she started to write! Her five children keep her on her toes. She has a very large dog who knocks everything over, a very small terrier who barks a lot and two cats. When time allows, Lynne is a keen gardener.

Books by Lynne Graham

Harlequin Presents

Indian Prince's Hidden Son

Conveniently Wed!

The Greek's Surprise Christmas Bride

Cinderella Brides for Billionaires

Cinderella's Royal Secret
The Italian in Need of an Heir

Innocent Christmas Brides

A Baby on the Greek's Doorstep
Christmas Babies for the Italian

Passion in Paradise

The Innocent's Forgotten Wedding

Visit the Author Profile page
at Harlequin.com for more titles.

Lynne Graham

THE GREEK'S CONVENIENT CINDERELLA

HARLEQUIN
PRESENTS

HARLEQUIN®
PRESENTS®

Recycling programs for this product may not exist in your area.

ISBN-13: 978-1-335-40334-6

The Greek's Convenient Cinderella

Copyright © 2021 by Lynne Graham

This edition published by arrangement with Harlequin Books S.A.

For questions and comments about the quality of this book, please contact us at CustomerService@Harlequin.com.

Harlequin Enterprises ULC
22 Adelaide St. West, 40th Floor
Toronto, Ontario M5H 4E3, Canada
www.Harlequin.com

Printed in U.S.A.

THE GREEK'S CONVENIENT CINDERELLA

CHAPTER ONE

EVERY EYE AROUND the crowded conference table locked in astonishment on to Althea Lekkas's exquisite face when she gasped. 'I'm sorry… I'm calling off the wedding!'

'You can't!' expostulated her father, Linus, jumping upright with knotted fists of fury. 'If you call it off this late in the day, I'll disown you!'

Jude Alexandris almost laughed at that melodramatic threat from his future father-in-law, who was embarrassingly keen for the marriage to take place. After all, the Alexandris billions were a living legend and Jude was accustomed to being regarded as a literal golden goose. Not that the huge weight and purchasing power of all that money had ever made anyone in *his* family happy, he acknowledged grimly.

His grandfather was a manipulative, bitter

old man who had outlived three wives. His father, an only child like Jude, had been a high-flyer in business but utterly useless on the husband and father front. His mother, Clio, discarded by her husband and denied her son, had thrown her broken heart into creating a world-famous garden and only there had she found some measure of contentment. Jude himself? He recalled being truly happy only once, when he was twenty-one and on top of the world because back then he had loved Althea, and had believed that she loved him. He had truly believed that he could ignore all the cynics and rewrite Alexandris family history.

Sadly, that naive hope hadn't lasted long. Althea had slept with another man, destroying everything he had ever felt for her and, seven years on, they were merely friends, who had agreed to marry for purely practical reasons. Thanks to his grandfather's machinations, and the pressure those had put on him, Jude needed a wife in a hurry and Althea, divorced in the wake of a short, disastrous marriage, craved the freedom from family expectations that a second marriage would give her.

As Althea burst into floods of tears, Jude stood up in one fluid motion to ask if there was an office free. He was very tall at six foot five, lean and muscular with the physique of an athlete. He cropped his riot of black curls short. Flaring ebony brows framed shrewd dark eyes set below lashes long and lush enough to make the average woman weep in envy. A beautiful child, he had grown into an even more beautiful man. Lean, sculpted features, sheathed in olive skin and worthy of a Greek god, completed the vision of a male who turned female heads wherever he went.

One of his English legal team rose in haste to accommodate Jude's request for a more private space and he urged Althea out of the room into one across the corridor.

'I didn't mean to just drop it on you like that…not in front of an audience!' Althea sobbed. 'But I *can't* go through with it! It would be wrong for me…maybe not for you, but for me.'

'Are you sure this isn't just wedding nerves?' Jude asked, leaning back against the door with the cool of a man who rarely lost control of his emotions.

This had been the day the prenuptial agreement was to be signed, and the wedding was to take place within the week. Jude would have been content with a quick civil ceremony, but Althea had wanted a big wedding, which had taken weeks of planning. Thanks to her insistence on all the glitzy trappings, he was now perilously close to the finishing line, which was only a couple of months away. If he didn't have a wife by his thirtieth birthday, his mother, Clio, would be forced to leave her home and her precious garden and there would be nothing he could do to forestall that blow and the devastation it would inflict on her. Unfortunately for Clio, she lived in an Alexandris family property, which Jude would only inherit after his grandfather passed away and his grandfather, Isidore, was using that as a threat to force his grandson into taking a wife. His mother might be a rather difficult personality but Jude still wanted to protect her.

'No, it's not nerves.' The slender blonde drew a tissue out of her bag and dabbed carefully at her eyes, struggling not to dislodge her fake lashes. 'I realised that I was marrying you for the wrong reasons, that I'd be looking for more than you were willing to give and that I wouldn't want to let you go at the end of it. That wouldn't be fair to you *or* me, so I'm backing out now because I do value your friendship and I don't want to lose that as well.

'No, don't say anything,' Althea muttered in a wobbly undertone as he studied her with a troubled frown, his wide, sensual mouth compressing at that explanation. 'I'm doing the right thing for both of us and you *know* it. You're never going to feel anything more for me than you do now. I killed all that when I slept with your best friend. And now I'm leaving you in a hell of a mess and Dad's going to go crazy about the wedding costs I've incurred.'

'I'll cover the expenses,' Jude interposed, reaching for her hand.

'You *can't*, not when I'm the one backing out of our agreement,' Althea protested, tugging her hand gently from his. 'I'm always screwing up, Jude.'

'No, you can blame me for this. I should never have told you what my grandfather was threatening to do in the first place.'

'We're friends. I offered, you didn't *ask* for my help,' Althea reminded him ruefully. 'No, this is on me. Blame it on my never quite getting over you and craving the kudos of walking down the aisle with you. That appealed to my vanity and I'm ashamed of it. You're not a trophy to be shown off.'

Registering that her reasons for not marrying him were *not* reasons he could argue with, Jude expelled his breath in a sharp hiss of grudging acceptance. 'Let's go back in and deal with the fallout.'

'But what are you going to do now?' Althea demanded, searching his face with a more calculating light in her gaze.

'Find me a wife…one without the finer sensibilities that persuaded you to back out on me,' he murmured wryly while fiercely resisting the urge to remonstrate with her about the feelings she was insisting she still cherished for him.

'You won't find anyone at this late stage,' Althea countered. 'You'd be wiser rethinking what you're willing to offer me.'

Jude almost groaned out loud because he had already offered Althea everything he was prepared to offer. Unfortunately, she was still on the rebound from a bad marriage, and fanciful. She ignored the reality that seven years earlier she would never have slept with another man in the first place had she genuinely loved him and that in any case these days they were no longer the boy and girl they had once been. She had been his first love, his *only* love, but fidelity was a hard limit for Jude and, although he had forgiven her as a friend, she had annihilated the deeper feelings he had once had for her. She didn't understand that, couldn't accept that bottom line, but then that was Althea, always wanting most what she couldn't have, always believing that a pretty gesture or the right words could work a miracle. Jude had always had a tougher and less idealistic outlook because his dysfunctional background had stolen his innocence when he was still very young.

His earliest memory was of his parents fighting over his father's extramarital affairs. He remembered his father's arrogant defiance and his mother's agonised hurt and hysterical recriminations. He was the unfortunate baby who had been christened Judas in the cradle by his embittered mother because she had first caught his father in another woman's bed shortly before she gave birth. In that moment, Jude had become the symbol of everything his mother had suffered, and he suspected that even now she had yet to manage to forgive him for it. His grandfather had despised his daughter-in-law and had renamed his grandson Jude and when, inevitably, there was a divorce, the older man had moved heaven and earth to ensure that Jude's father was awarded full custody of his son and that his mother saw as little as possible of her child as he grew up.

'You're an Alexandris male,' Clio had told Jude during one of her brief visits. 'It's written in your genes that you'll lie and cheat with women just like your father. You won't be able to help yourself.'

But, Jude was a natural rebel. As soon as he'd been told that, he had sworn that he would not repeat his father's mistakes. After all, he had grown up with the consequences of his father's inability to maintain a stable relationship with any woman. He had had several stepmothers and his absentee father had taken countless lovers as well. Ironically, his father had never loved any woman the way he had loved Jude's mother, but he had been far too proud to admit that even to himself. Dion Alexandris had lived a life full of thrills and spills, ultimately dying in a racing accident in a car he should not have been driving.

Jude was equally volatile, but he also had his mother's common sense and his grandfather's cool, cutting intellect, and he was a renowned 'fixer' in the business world, possessing that rare ability to rise above ego and emotion and see right to the heart of a matter to find a solution to complex problems.

Jude was on the way out of the office when one of his legal team members addressed him. 'What will you do now?'

He glanced down with a frown at the smaller man, struggling to recall his name while remaining disconcerted that a junior executive would approach him in such a familiar fashion. *'Cherchez la femme,'* he responded drily.

Calvin Hetherington squared his slight shoulders. Although he was not tall, he had the smooth, blond, boyish good looks of a fashion model. 'What you need is a woman you can pay to marry you and who won't make a fuss when you walk away.'

'Is that so?' Jude said discouragingly.

'I know someone who wouldn't cause you any trouble, who would marry you for a set fee.'

'I'm sure I can find a gold-digger of my own,' Jude murmured flatly.

'But you need someone discreet, someone willing to stick to *your* rules, not a spoiled and privileged woman from your world,' the older man contended. 'Someone who will do it for a price without hassle or consequences.'

It was a compelling truth even if Jude wasn't in the mood to listen to it. 'And where am I likely to find this wonder woman?' he prompted drily.

A card was settled into his empty hand. 'Ring me if you decide you're interested.'

'Who is she?' Jude demanded impatiently.

'My stepdaughter. I want her out of my home because my girlfriend won't move in until *she* moves *out*,' Calvin offered with a wry roll of his eyes. 'But Tansy has no money, no job.'

'Not my problem, not in my interests either,' Jude sliced in with ruthless bite as he strode into the lift, thrusting the card into his pocket while reflecting that occasionally you met some real weirdos, although he had not expected to discover that even a junior member of his British legal team fell into that category. Where had that presumptuous idiot got the idea that he could freely suggest some random young woman as a bride for Jude?

Jude, who had grown up knowing that because of his unlimited wealth he could marry virtually *any* woman he set his sights on. He wasn't desperate enough to consider settling on a complete stranger…was he?

No, of course, he wasn't. Yet the seductive suggestion of a woman who would play by his rules and provide him with no unwelcome surprises could only linger with him in the wake of that messy denouement with Althea. Someone he paid to marry him, someone who had no personal stake in the marriage other than enrichment, he mused. Yes, that option *would* suit him best, a woman without her own agenda, a woman without personal feelings involved in the exchange, a woman who would simply marry him because he paid her handsomely to do so.

Even better, such a woman could be dispensed with as soon as he was able…easily, casually and without consequences. Yes, although Jude might not have appreciated his timing, Hetherington, he thought, glancing down at the card to get the name, had actually made a valid point. Simple guidelines and goals often worked the best. After all, he had already screwed up badly when he'd chosen to rely on Althea and their supposed friendship. Althea had made it all personal and emotional while Jude had seen absolutely no reason why emotion should figure in any part of the arrangement. A woman who could see that truth as clearly as he did would be his perfect match.

Jude had already reached a decision when he strode back into his opulent penthouse apartment. He had to consider *every* option before he ran out of time and that meant checking out the gold-digger possibility. He rang Hetherington. 'I'm willing to meet your stepdaughter,' he said flatly. 'Set up a meeting.'

Tansy scooped her dripping, wriggling baby sister out of the bath and wrapped her securely in a towel. Her stepfather was calling her from downstairs and, holding Posy deftly on her hip, she walked out to the landing. 'I'll be down as soon as I've got Posy settled,' she called back.

Posy tried to roll away while her big sister was slotting her into a fresh onesie, but Tansy was practised at dealing with her playfulness. In spite of her difficult start in life, at ten months old and blessed with a mop of blond curls and big blue eyes, Posy was a very pretty baby with a happy disposition. Sadly, Tansy and Posy's mother had died within minutes of bringing her second daughter into the world. At the hospital, reeling in shock from that tragedy, Tansy had taken one look into her sister's eyes and had realised that, although she didn't like her stepfather very much, she would never be able to walk away from her newborn sibling.

And yet her life, she conceded ruefully, would have been so much easier if she *had* had the strength to walk away.

Her aunt, Violet, had given her some surprisingly hard-hearted advice after her mother's funeral. 'Leave now and go back to that university course that your mother made you abandon. That baby is your sister, *not* your daughter. By all means, stay in touch with her and your stepfather, but let them get on with their lives while you return to yours. You don't owe them or your mother's memory anything more than that.'

But, unfortunately, nothing was that simple or straightforward, particularly when feelings got involved, Tansy conceded ruefully. Posy might not be Tansy's daughter, but Tansy had become as deeply attached to her baby sister as any new mother. Calvin had asked Tansy to stay on to look after Posy and enable him to return to work and she had agreed to that, but she had soon begun to feel taken for granted as an unpaid childminder, and then her stepfather had begun dating again. While acknowledging that Calvin was only in his early thirties, having been considerably younger than her mother, Tansy had still thought his interest in other women had returned tastelessly soon, but she had minded her own business when Calvin's lady friends had begun to stay over for the night. Only when Calvin had begun to pressure his regular girlfriend, Susie, into taking over Posy's care and replacing Tansy had Tansy interfered, because it had quickly become painfully obvious that Susie was too irresponsible to take charge of a baby.

One afternoon Susie had actually gone out and left Tansy's little sister alone and unattended in the house when something more entertaining than childcare had been offered to her. There had been other incidents as well, incidents that bordered on child neglect, which had stoked Tansy's growing concern for her sister's welfare.

It was not as though she could trust Posy's father to look out for his child's welfare. In fact, Calvin Hetherington hadn't the smallest interest in being a father to his motherless daughter, nor did he seem to have developed any natural affection for his child. He had married Tansy's mother, Rosie, a successful businesswoman in her mid-forties, and the last thing he had expected out of that union was to become a parent. Rosie might have been overjoyed by her unforeseen pregnancy, but Calvin had been aghast and his wife's death had not made him any keener to take on a paternal role. He might live in the same household but he behaved as though his daughter did not exist. That was why Tansy had stayed on to look after her sister even though her stepfather had recently made it rather obvious that he thought it was time she moved out.

In her will, her mother had left both her home and her beauty salon to her second husband. Had it not been for her infant sibling and her impoverished state Tansy would immediately have moved out because she felt very much surplus to requirements in Calvin's home life now that he was entertaining other women.

'Is the kid in bed?' Calvin checked as Tansy walked into the spacious lounge. 'Look, sit down. We have to talk.'

'What about?' Tansy enquired defensively, standing straight and stiff, instinctively distrustful of the vain, shallow and selfish man her mother had chosen to marry. She had to force herself to sit down and act relaxed and pleasant, which she had learned to do around her stepfather.

'I'm going to be totally honest with you. I'm facing bankruptcy proceedings in the near future,' the slim blond man informed her as he stood at the window.

Tansy froze and paled. 'That's not possible. For goodness's sake, you only sold Mum's business a couple of months ago,' she reminded him.

Calvin Hetherington sighed. 'The beauty parlour was up to its neck in debt—'

'It was a thriving business!' Tansy argued in startled disagreement.

'*Was* being the operative word, Tansy. Your mother was off work for months during her pregnancy and the business went downhill, even though you tried to pick up the slack. Any money your mother made, she spent on extending the property, hiring more staff or buying new equipment,' Calvin enumerated impatiently. 'There were no savings, nothing put by for leaner times. I had to sell, and the price was swallowed by the debts the business had accrued. Then there's the mortgage on this house.'

Tansy frowned in consternation. 'There's a mortgage on this house?'

'The price of all the improvements your mother insisted on making. I could lecture you for an hour on the financial cost of your mother's passing. I'm afraid we always lived above our means, juggling overdrafts and debts,' Calvin admitted grudgingly. 'I'm sure that you realised that your mother really only liked the finer things in life?'

Tansy pinned her parted lips mutinously closed. While it was true that she had often thought her mother had rather extravagant tastes she had also never heard Calvin complain about their comfortable lifestyle or seek to cut back on the expenses of their fancy cars and even flashier holidays. 'Bankruptcy though?' she breathed starkly, avoiding a pointless exchange of bestowing blame for the debts he had mentioned. 'That's a very serious step—'

'Yes and, unfortunately, this house will have to be sold as well. I don't want to see Posy deprived of her only home.' Calvin sighed heavily. 'But there is another option... a rather strange and unexpected option that has literally dropped right into our laps and which could be the answer to all our problems.'

Tansy sat forward, her green eyes locked to him with brimming curiosity. 'What option would that be?'

'My firm's richest client needs a wife for business purposes, and he's prepared to pay a lot of money to the right candidate.'

'What kind of business purposes?' Tansy pressed suspiciously.

'I'm not in possession of that information. Jude Alexandris is a very private man. He doesn't explain his motivations to his solicitors,' her stepfather told her.

'Does he need a British passport or something?'

'I very much doubt it. But I do know that

he needs a fake wife. It would be a marriage of convenience. Sign up for it and the sky will be the limit for you,' Calvin told her with a sudden surge of enthusiasm. 'Not only will he pay a large sum of money up front if you agree to marry him, but he will also make a very substantial settlement on you after the divorce and ensure that you never have to work again.'

'That sounds like a winning scheme for a gold-digger,' Tansy pointed out sweetly. 'But I'm not that way inclined. Of course, I can see the appeal from your side of the fence. Presumably if I agree to this nonsense, *you* would get the large sum of money upfront to settle your debts and retain your lifestyle.'

'Think of the benefits for Posy,' her step-father urged speciously.

'Calvin, you don't give two hoots about Posy or her needs. You're only thinking about saving your own skin,' Tansy countered rue-fully.

Calvin frowned. 'You know that's not true. I love that little girl.'

'No, you don't,' Tansy said with regret. 'You live in the same house and you haven't bothered to even see her in over a week. I'm not judging you for that. I accept that not everyone wants to be a parent but what worries me the most is that you don't care about her welfare either.'

'And how do you make that out?' Calvin riposted, angry colour spotting his cheeks at that criticism.

'Well, you keep on pushing Posy off on your girlfriend even though it's perfectly obvious that Susie hasn't an ounce of interest in acting as her substitute mother.'

'Posy is *my* daughter,' her stepfather reminded her with lethal timing. 'Allow me to decide what's best for her. Now what about this proposition? Don't ignore the fact that there would be substantial benefits in the marriage for you as well.'

'But nothing that I value. Yes, money would make it easier for me to move on with my life and possibly return to university,' Tansy conceded reluctantly, 'but it wouldn't sort out the problem of who is to care for Posy. Right now, I think I'm the best person to look after my sister because I love her. Why can't you sign over custody of Posy to me?'

Calvin studied her in indignant disbelief. 'And what would people think of me if I did something like that? Handing my own flesh and blood over to a girl barely into her twenties?'

'Is that all you care about? What other people think?' Tansy viewed him with helpless contempt. 'At the end of the day what should matter to you is what makes *Posy* happy and secure.'

'Well, it certainly won't be you when you're broke and living under my roof at my expense,' her stepfather reminded her crushingly. 'You have no means of supporting a child, no income, no home—'

Tansy jumped to her feet with knotted fists. 'There's nothing I wouldn't do to keep Posy!' she snapped back at him angrily. 'Given a little time I could find us a home and I could find a job—'

'Marrying Jude Alexandris would give you a home *and* an income,' Calvin pointed out persuasively. 'You just said that there's *nothing* you wouldn't do to keep Posy. Did you mean it? If you agree to marry Alexandris, I'll consider giving you custody of Posy. In those circumstances, nobody would question me handing her over to you because you would be in a position to offer her so much *more* than I ever could. The Alexandris family are one of the richest in the world—'

'Are you serious?' Tansy gasped in complete astonishment at the suggestion that should she be willing to agree to such a marriage he might be willing to surrender his rights to her sister.

'Yes, you agree to marry Alexandris and hand over that initial sum of money to me and I will agree to relinquish my paternal rights in your favour. But, mind you, it won't be that easy,' Calvin told her, switching into cool, curt business mode. 'You would have to impress Alexandris first and you won't do that by mouthing off to him the way you do to me. He will have a low tolerance level for insolence because he's not accustomed to dealing with it. I wouldn't suggest telling him about Posy in advance either as he will only see a young child accompanying you as a problem and a burden. He wants a yes-woman who will do as she's told, nothing more demanding.'

Tansy let his words wash over her while she breathed in deep and slow. A yes-woman, well, she supposed she had been a weak yes-person for much of her life, constantly striving to please and impress her mother and never quite managing to make the grade. From childhood, Tansy had been a disappointment to Rosie Browne. She had cried when her mother had entered her in beauty pageants, come over all shy when she'd got her a booking as a child model and had failed utterly in the drama and ballet classes that had followed.

It was that sad history, that awareness of past failure, that had made Tansy take time out of the radiography degree her mother had denigrated and come to the older woman's aid when she had asked for her help while she was pregnant. Just for once, Tansy had wanted to succeed in winning her mother's approval because she had badly needed the comfort of believing that in spite of everything she could still be a *good* daughter. Regrettably, she had no memory whatsoever of her father, who had died when she was a baby, and by the time her mother had married Calvin, she had been fifteen years old. He had had no desire to take on a stepfather role and she and Calvin had pretty much avoided each other until she went to university. Currently, she struggled to deal with Calvin without her mother around because everything about superficial, smooth-talking, selfish Calvin irritated her.

'You will be seeing Alexandris tomorrow morning at ten for an interview,' Calvin informed her, startling her with that announcement. 'I'll organise Susie to look after the baby.'

'Tomorrow?' Tansy gasped.

'We have no time to lose and neither has he. He's on a tight timeline. I need to coach you on what Alexandris expects so that you'll impress him as a viable choice,' her stepfather decreed, disconcerting her even more.

Tansy was taken aback by the concept of being 'coached' by Calvin in anything. Was she even willing to go through some marriage ceremony with a stranger for money? Put that baldly, it struck her as a proposition that only a greedy, unscrupulous woman would even consider, and she was neither of those things. On the other hand, if agreeing to that proposition gave Tansy the right to ensure that her little sister was never again left screaming, hungry and unwashed in her cot, she had to think again about what she was ready to sacrifice to achieve a greater good.

'Will you promise me that if this guy agrees

to marry me, you will hand over Posy?' she pressed worriedly. 'Because that would be the only reason I am even prepared to consider this idea.'

'So you say,' Calvin jibed with a curied lip. 'But I refuse to accept that the cash and the lifestyle Alexandris could give you doesn't feature in your decision.'

'If this works and you get the money for me doing this, are you willing to sign over custody of Posy to me?' Tansy demanded a second time, needing that reassurance.

'Tansy, if you can pull this off, I'd sign my soul over to the devil, never mind give up Posy,' Calvin admitted with unusual honesty. 'Right now, I'm facing disaster and I'll do anything to avoid it…'

CHAPTER TWO

TANSY AVERTED HER gaze from her reflection in the mirrored lift wafting her up to the penthouse apartment. She was still a little shaken by the elaborate security checks she had had to undergo to prove her identity on the ground floor and gain access to the building. She was now in a special lift that travelled only to the penthouse apartment, a luxury that impressed her to death with its sheer exclusivity. In truth, getting permission to even enter the presence of Jude Alexandris felt like an achievement of no mean order.

Maybe she didn't look quite fancy enough to impress, she conceded ruefully. Maybe she should have tailored her appearance to exactly what Calvin had advised and trowelled on the make-up and used every beautician trick known to her to ensure the ultimate polished finish. Unfortunately, that extremely groomed look wasn't Tansy and never had been. Although her mother had ensured that her vanity-resistant daughter was taught every cosmetic skill available, Tansy had never enjoyed the artificial aspect of presenting herself as someone she felt she was not.

For that reason, Tansy was only wearing light make-up, but she was also, at Calvin's behest, wearing a dress and shoes she felt would have been more suitable for clubbing than a supposed interview. The last time she had worn the short green dress and perilously high heels had been to dance at her friend Laura's wedding and she had been a different girl back then, she thought sadly.

Only eighteen months ago, she had still been at university studying radiography and looking forward to the hospital career she had planned. And then without warning everything had gone pear-shaped. Her mother's pregnancy had been problematic from the outset and when Rosie had found herself struggling to run her beauty salon it had been her daughter she had turned to for help and support. At the time, Tansy had assumed she would only need a couple of months out of her course and that once her sibling was born she would be free to return to her studies. Yet even now, when she accepted that that miscalculation had concluded her education, nothing could make her regret her sister's birth, she conceded fondly. Sometimes life demanded sudden changes of direction and she had simply had to come to terms with the different path that had opened up ahead of her. And if that meant marrying some weird, rich foreigner, she *would* cope if it was for Posy's essential benefit.

With a soft bell tone, the lift doors whirred back and exposed a vast expanse of marble floor flooded by light from the glass roof overhead. A single metal sculpture took pride of place to one side of a glass hall table. It was very stark décor, but it also struck a highly sophisticated note. Tansy stepped out of the lift just as an older woman in a severe black dress appeared from a doorway.

'Miss Browne, please come this way,' she urged, leading the way into a breathtaking reception area flooded with light and surrounded by fabulous panoramic views of London.

Indeed, so spectacular was that space that Tansy didn't even notice that the older woman had abandoned her or that, as she pirouetted round on one high heel to better appreciate what lay beyond the wall of window glass, a tall man had strolled in off the roof terrace behind her.

Jude studied his visitor with appreciative eyes. She was a beauty and a surprisingly un-usual one, distinctly different from the common herd. Broadly speaking, she had blond hair, but it was streaked in shades that ran from light brown to gold to pale honey and it looked as natural as her delicately pointed features. Her hair fell halfway down her back in a thick mass of rather messy waves. She wore a raincoat over a dress that revealed legs that in shape and length would not have shamed a Las Vegas showgirl. Slender in build, she was of medium height. Against her creamy skin, her almond-shaped green eyes glowed as clear as emeralds above her full soft pink mouth.

'Jude Alexandris…' Jude murmured, think-ing, yes, she would fit his purpose, *more* than match and make possible that extra dimen-sion to the marriage that he had originally planned with Althea.

After all, why go to all the trouble of getting married to satisfy and silence his grand-father's demands and not take advantage of that legal union? It would make sense to try to have a child with the woman he married and, in so doing, shift his cantankerous grand-father into long-overdue retirement, which would leave Jude free to live his life and run the Alexandris empire exactly as he liked without interference from anyone. When Althea had bowed out, he had given up on the idea of a child but why should he do that? A woman prepared to marry for money would probably have little compunction about pro-viding him with a child in return for an even richer payday.

At the unexpected sound of another voice, Tansy flinched and jumped and spun round, her coat flying out to catch on the small table beside her and toppling it. 'Oh, for heaven's sake,' she began in incredulous embarrass-ment, wobbling on the high heels that she had not worn in well over a year, one foot semi-skidding on the tiled floor, making her lurch clumsily to one side.

Jude caught her upper arm with a powerful hand to steady her before she could fall and picked up the table with the other. 'Sorry, I didn't mean to startle you,' he drawled.

Tansy froze as his hand dropped from her arm again and he backed off several feet. 'I got lost in the view. I was picking out landmarks like a total tourist,' she confessed unevenly, because in reality even contriving to breathe that close to such a perfect vision of masculinity challenged her.

She had looked him up on the Internet, of course, she had, and could hardly have failed to notice his classic good looks. In the flesh, however, he fell into another category entirely, she thought helplessly, ensnared as she was by stunning dark eyes surrounded by a spectacular fringe of black lashes. In real life, he was as visually dazzling as a golden angel springing to sudden life from a printed page. Quite literally, Jude Alexandris took her breath away. His lean, darkly handsome features were as flawless as his bronzed skin tone, his incredible height as striking as his lean, muscular physique. She had felt his strength when he'd grabbed her before she could tumble over in her stupid heels and even that strength of his had made her go weak at the knees, burying every brain cell she possessed...

And that swiftly, Tansy burned with mortification because if there was one thing she never allowed herself to be with a man it was gullible. Being weak and impressionable had got her heart broken and her trust in the opposite sex smashed when she was only nineteen. The experience had hurt like hell and she had never quite recovered from it or regained her youthful confidence. Ever since then, though, she had been careful to avoid the attention of the kind of good-looking man who was a promiscuous sleaze beneath the superficial charm. And she knew Jude Alexandris was a legendary womaniser because not one of the photos she had seen of him online in female company had featured the *same* woman twice. He changed his bed partners as often as other men changed their socks and, naturally, so experienced a guy was fully aware of the pulling power of his extraordinary physical attraction.

'Mr Alexandris,' Tansy pronounced rather stiffly.

'Come and sit down,' he invited lazily. 'Tea or coffee?'

'Coffee, please,' Tansy said, following him round a sectional room divider into a rather more intimate space furnished with sumptuous sofas, and sinking down into the comfortable depths of one, her tense spine rigorously protesting that amount of relaxation.

She was fighting to get a grip on her composure again, but nothing about Jude Alexandris in the flesh matched the formal online images she had viewed. He wasn't wearing a sharply cut business suit, he was wearing faded, ripped and worn jeans that outlined long powerful thighs and narrow hips and accentuated the prowling natural grace of his every movement. An equally casual dark grey cotton top complemented the jeans. One sleeve was partially pushed up to reveal a strong brown forearm and a small tattoo that appeared to be printed letters of some sort. His garb reminded her that, although he might be older than her, he was still only in his late twenties and that, unlike her, he had felt no need to dress to impress.

Her pride stung at the knowledge that she was little more than a commodity on Alexandris's terms. Either he would choose her, or he wouldn't. She had put herself on the market to be bought though, she thought with sudden self-loathing. How could she blame Jude Alexandris for her stepfather's use of virtual blackmail to get her agreement? Everything she was doing was for Posy, she reminded herself squarely, and the end would justify the means...*wouldn't it?*

'So...' Tansy remarked in a stilted tone because she was determined not to sit there acting like the powerless person she knew herself to be in his presence. 'You require a fake wife...'

Jude shifted a broad shoulder in a very slight shrug. 'Only we would know it was fake. It would have to seem real to everyone else from the start to the very end,' he advanced calmly. 'Everything between us would have to remain confidential.'

'I'm not a gossip, Mr Alexandris.' In fact Tansy almost laughed at the idea of even having anyone close enough to confide in, because she had left her friends behind at university and certainly none of them had seemed to understand her decision to make herself responsible for her baby sister rather than return to the freedom of student life.

'I trust no one,' Jude countered without

apology. 'You would be legally required to sign a non-disclosure agreement before I married you.'

'Understood. My stepfather explained that to me,' Tansy acknowledged, her attention reluctantly drawn to his careless sprawl on the opposite sofa, the long, muscular line of a masculine thigh straining against well-washed denim. Her head tipped back, her colour rising as she made herself look at his face instead, encountering glittering dark eyes that made the breath hitch in her throat.

'I find you attractive too,' Jude Alexandris murmured as though she had spoken.

'I don't know what you're talking about,' Tansy protested, the faint pink in her cheeks heating exponentially as her tummy flipped while she wondered if she truly could be read that easily by a man.

'For this to work, we would need that physical attraction. Nobody is likely to be fooled by two strangers pretending what they don't feel, least of all my family, some of whom are shrewd judges of character.'

Tansy had paled. 'Why would we need attraction? I assumed this was to be a marriage on paper, nothing more.'

'Then you assumed wrong,' Jude told her without skipping a beat. 'Neither your stepfather nor any of my legal team are aware of the personal terms I require for this to work. There was no need for them to have access to that knowledge because I had already reached agreement in private with the woman I believed I was going to marry.'

'Your friend…who…er…let you down,' Tansy mumbled, playing for time while she struggled to absorb what he was telling her. 'Perhaps you should be sharing those personal terms with me now.'

'That was always my intention…if you met the initial requirements,' Jude responded calmly.

Tansy was shaken by the discovery that Calvin had not, actually, been privy to the finer details of the marriage of convenience he had told her about, although he had talked with his usual aplomb as though he knew everything. Of course, it had all sounded too good to be true, she reflected ruefully, all that money upfront just to pretend to be the wife of a very rich man.

'Sex *would* feature,' Jude informed her without a shade of discomfiture. 'For as long as we would be together it would be a normal marriage.'

'I'm afraid that would be a deal-breaker for me,' Tansy responded stiffly. 'I wasn't aware that intimacy would be involved in this arrangement, nor do I understand why it should even have to be.'

'This marriage may well need to last a couple of years. I'm not prepared to be celibate for that length of time. But if I satisfy my needs with another woman, my family will be immediately aware that the marriage is a fake because it is widely known that I believe in marital fidelity,' Jude explained with the same cool that somehow made her want to slap him, trip him up, in some way jolt him, because his complete calm and control while she was embarrassed and flustered infuriated her.

He believed in marital fidelity? Tansy wanted to scoff, and only with difficulty did she keep her tongue clamped in her mouth. No man who bedded as many different women as he did could possibly believe in marital fidelity! Who did he think he was kidding? Did she really look that credulous?

'Look, I wasn't aware of your…er…terms,'

Tansy framed awkwardly, rising with difficulty in her high heels from the sofa, clutching at the arm to steady herself. 'There's no point in you telling me any more as I couldn't agree to what you've just suggested.'

Jude sprang upright as well. 'Are you serious? You're saying no, over something as trivial as sex?'

Her heart-shaped face reddened. 'It's not trivial to me.'

'Is there someone else in your life? Some reason why you're taking that attitude?' Jude probed because, the more he looked at her, the more interested he became, and he could not credit that she would turn him down. No woman had ever turned him down and he had already felt the appreciative weight of her eyes on him, had recognised that spark of mutual attraction for what it was. That streak of individuality he had recognised in her at first glimpse further appealed to him.

'I'd sooner not get into that,' Tansy muttered, stepping back as the older woman swept in with a tray and laid it down on the coffee table. 'But it wouldn't work for me...'

As his housekeeper departed again, Jude recognised Tansy's awkwardness and found it as oddly appealing a trait as the long coltish legs she didn't seem to know what to do with. He gazed down at her, watching her worry at her full lower lip with the edge of her teeth in a nervous gesture and glance up at him from below curling lashes. It wasn't staged and he found it incredibly sexy and he didn't know why——didn't know why it should send a current of primal lust to his groin that made him hard as stone within seconds.

'We could make it work,' he heard himself declare. 'Sit down. We'll talk about this.'

'There's really no point when I'd be wasting your time,' Tansy mumbled, casting a longing look in the direction of the lift.

'Tell me why it would be a deal-breaker for you. I'm curious,' Jude admitted. 'These days everyone is so casual about sex.'

'Not everyone,' Tansy argued, sitting down very stiffly, only staying because he had blocked her path of escape and she didn't want to come across as childish and immature.

He spread fluid brown hands. 'Explain,' he pressed with genuine curiosity.

Tansy lifted her chin although she could feel heat gathering below her skin, but she refused to be intimidated by Jude Alexandris. He was gorgeous and he was rich but neither of those things made him any better than she was. 'I'm a virgin. I didn't plan it that way, but the right guy never came along,' she framed curtly. 'I do, however, know he's not going to be you in some mockery of a marriage.'

His black brows drew together and he knew the very minute she spoke that he *was* going to be *that* guy, no matter what it cost him, no matter how hard he had to work to achieve it. He was an Alexandris: it was ingrained in his DNA to want what anyone told him he couldn't have, and he had wanted her the minute he'd laid eyes on her. He didn't understand why, because she was by no means perfect and he could see that she had a slight overbite and a nose that turned up a little at the tip, giving her a faintly impish expression. And he usually went for blondes and she wasn't blonde, not properly blonde, and yet that streaky, unruly mane of hers kept on grabbing his attention as the light glimmered over the differing shades. A virgin, though. That possibility hadn't even occurred to him with a woman of almost twenty-three, particularly one he had already deemed to be a gold-digger. When had he become so cynical that he expected all young women to be cookie-cutter copies of each other?

'The marriage won't be a mockery and no woman with me will ever be treated with less than respect,' Jude countered levelly. 'Obviously, I would give you time to get to know me. After all, once we're married, neither one of us will be straying very far from the other in the first few months.'

Tansy reddened even more, unwarily connecting with those tawny golden eyes locked to her, feeling the butterflies leap and jump in her tummy, her nipples snap tight inside her bra, horrendously aware of that attraction she couldn't deny or stop in its tracks. 'It's not possible, just not possible,' she proclaimed uncomfortably, shifting a hand in denial when he offered her the coffee on the tray, his manners impeccable even in a tense moment. 'I'm sorry for wasting your time.'

Jude was astonished by her determined departure. Firstly, people never walked out on him before *he* had finished with them. Secondly, people generally bent over backwards to please him. Thirdly, the female sex in particular were his biggest fans.

His long powerful stride caught him up with her before she could step into the waiting lift. He reached for her hand. 'We could make this work,' he told her levelly. 'Give me your phone.'

'Why?'

'So that you can contact me when you change your mind,' Jude responded.

'Are you always this confident?' Tansy unlocked her phone and gave it to him solely to be polite.

Brilliant dark golden eyes raked her troubled face as he punched in the number. 'Always.'

As Tansy vanished into the lift, Jude was perplexed, striving to understand her behaviour, because it didn't make the smallest sense that a woman willing to marry him for money would baulk at the inclusion of a little sex. A venal nature was rarely accompanied by much in the way of finer feelings. As a rule, Jude had discovered, gold-diggers were very single-minded, willing to do and say anything and deceive anyone to enrich themselves. Could she really be a virgin or was that some kind of ruse? His suspicious nature was honed by having been for years a prime target of female manipulative wiles.

Tansy travelled home on the train in a daze. She couldn't possibly have agreed to sleep with him, could she? That would have been indecent, she assured herself, and yet the closer she got to home, the more apprehensive she became about the decision she had made. She would lie to Calvin when he asked, she decided. She would say Jude had said she wasn't suitable. It was perfectly understandable that she wasn't willing to go to bed with Jude Alexandris just to secure her baby sister's future...wasn't it? It wasn't as though he were unattractive, however, wasn't as though she were hanging on to her inexperience for any particular reason. It would be more truthful and accurate to say that confronted with the unexpected—the sex—she had panicked and fled.

In the event, what to tell Calvin Hetherington no longer mattered when he jerked open the front door at her approach and glowered at her. 'You told Alexandris *no*? You turned him down?' he roared at her in disbelief.

Tansy paled. 'Don't shout…you'll upset Posy.'

'Susie's taken her out to the park.'

'How did you find out I said no?' Tansy asked flatly.

'I rang him to ask how it went…and you blew it, for some crazy reason, *you blew it*!' Calvin snapped at her furiously. 'He was willing to proceed, you *weren't*. What happened? What are you playing at?' her stepfather demanded in a rage.

Recognising that Jude had protected his own privacy, Tansy shrugged. 'We just didn't gel.'

'Well, too bad for you!' her enraged stepfather launched back at her. 'You can go upstairs right now and pack and get out.'

'Get out?' Tansy echoed in shock.

'Why would I let you stay on here after you've wrecked the best opportunity we were ever going to get of saving this situation?' he slammed back at her, full of rancour.

'Because I look after your daughter and the house,' Tansy reminded him gently.

Calvin studied her with hard, resentful eyes. 'Susie will take care of both from now on. Go on, pack… I want you *out* before the end of the day!'

Tansy went upstairs on wooden legs and collapsed down on the edge of the bed. That was the moment that it dawned on her that she had no rights whatsoever in the situation she was in. She had no right to stay on in the house, which had originally been bought by her own father, because it now belonged wholly to Calvin and she wasn't a tenant. She had no right to interfere in Calvin's care arrangements for his daughter either because she was only a half-sister.

Susie would be free and unsupervised to do as she liked with the little girl. She could lose her temper and shout at Posy and slap her when she cried. Tansy shuddered at that memory. She could leave Posy unchanged in her cot whenever she liked and for as long as she liked, walk away while the child was in the bath, careless of her safety, and feed her inappropriate food because there wasn't going to be anyone around to object.

Tansy's chest went hollow at the thought of the baby she loved being subjected to such treatment round the clock. Susie didn't mean to be cruel, she was just too immature to be looking after a baby that wasn't her own, but she was also too much in love with Tansy's stepfather and too keen to move in with him to admit that unwelcome truth. It would be Posy who suffered for Tansy's refusal to consider having a 'normal' marriage with Jude Alexandris.

Her bedroom door was thrust open and two suitcases were set down firmly in front of her. 'It's best you go,' Calvin told her curtly. 'I could never forgive you for this.'

As he slammed the door behind him again, Tansy pulled out her phone and agonised while she looked for Jude's number in her contacts. She couldn't find it until she read 'future husband' in the list, and almost spontaneously combusted in rage because there was ordinary confidence and then there was the kind of glaring discordant confidence that made a woman want to run over a man with a steamroller to painfully squash the attitude and bravado out of him. And that was Jude's variety.

She called the number. 'Hello? Would that be future husband I'm addressing?'

'I don't know. Am I?' Jude enquired, not one whit surprised, it seemed, by her callback.

'That would have to be a yes,' Tansy bit out between clenched teeth. 'If you still want me to marry you, I'll agree.'

'We still have more to discuss,' Jude retorted crisply.

Tansy breathed in sustaining air fast and hard and wondered what it was about him that filled her with such irritation and rage. It wasn't reasonable. She might find his marital terms offensive and unpalatable, but he had presented them calmly and politely. It was not *his* fault that Calvin had tied her up in knots over Posy's future. It was not *his* fault that she loved her half-sister as much as if she had given birth to her, which was hardly surprising when she had been looking after the child since the day of her birth. Like any new mother, Tansy had done the sleepless nights, the anxiety attacks and fears that she was doing something wrong, and then the moments of pure gold when she looked down at Posy and her heart just threatened to burst with sheer love.

'When do you want to see me again?'

'This afternoon at my office. I don't have time to waste,' Jude told her with audible impatience. 'I'll text you the address. Come as soon as you can—I'll fit you in.'

Not very gracious, Tansy mused, her face burning as she kicked off the shoes and tore off the dress. The deal was done now, so it didn't matter what she wore, did it? She pulled on a stretchy, comfy skirt and teamed it with flat ankle boots and a floral top before putting on her coat and heading downstairs to see her stepfather again.

'I've agreed to marry him... OK?' she proclaimed as she stood in the living room doorway. 'So you'll need to make legal arrangements for Posy coming to live with me... I should tell Jude Alexandris about her now.'

Calvin vaulted upright, taken aback by her change of heart but visibly energised by the news. '*No!* You can't risk it. Why would he want a baby in the picture and all the noise and inconvenience that go with her?' he demanded. 'Use your brain, Tansy. Don't be a fool! The kid could make him back out. You can't afford to tell him about Posy until that wedding ring is safely on your finger.'

Tansy swallowed hard at that advice because honesty came more naturally to her than lying by omission, but if that was what it would take to safely and legally remove her sister from her father's mediocre care, she would do it. That penthouse apartment was huge and could probably absorb a couple of hidden babies without causing anyone any annoyance, she thought ruefully. There was no reason why Posy's existence should impact that much on Jude, she told herself firmly, squashing that memory of him saying that they would scarcely be apart the first few months of their marriage and reminding herself that she was marrying him for Posy's sake, which meant that Posy's interests had to come first and ahead of everything else. Even ahead of honesty and fair-mindedness? a little voice nagged in the back of her brain, but she silenced it because she couldn't afford to make a mistake when it came to Posy's future well-being.

Alexandris Industries occupied a landmark skyscraper in the City of London. By the time Tansy made it to the top floor, she was wishing she owned more formal clothes because her casual, youthful outfit seemed out of place. Her wardrobe, however, was depressingly slender because she hadn't had the money to add anything to it since her mother's demise and had never had cause to own dressier outfits.

The receptionist signalled Tansy with a discreet lift of her hand while she sat in the waiting area. Tansy stood up. 'Mr Alexandris will see you now…he has squeezed you in. Are you one of his godchildren?' the young woman asked, curiosity brimming in her keen gaze.

'No,' Tansy replied, reckoning that absolutely nobody would pick her unimpressive, rather ordinary self out as his future wife.

She was shown into a very large and empty office and ushered over to a sofa in the corner where coffee already awaited her. After a couple of minutes alone, she helped herself and tried to relax. When Jude blew through another door like a tornado ten minutes later, she almost dropped her cup as he strode towards her, unnervingly different and formal this time in a dark designer suit that fitted his lean, muscular physique to perfection. Yet that restive, powerful energy of his still fizzed in the air like a storm warning.

'Tansy…your name is rather unusual,' he remarked, disconcerting her with that opening greeting.

'For a couple of generations all the children on my mother's side of the family were named after plants or trees,' Tansy told him with a reluctant smile. 'All the obvious names for girls like Violet and Rosie and Daisy had already been used by the time I arrived.'

'A charming tradition,' Jude commented, his attention lingering on her, taking in the delicate curves beneath the close-fitting top, the long slender legs crossed, the feet in shabby boots. 'You look like a teenager in that outfit. I'll be accused of cradle robbing by the press—'

'Hardly. I'm almost twenty-three,' Tansy cut in defensively.

'I'm twenty-nine. It's still a big gap,' Jude told her stubbornly.

'If you say so.' *Yes-woman, yes-woman*, Tansy chanted soothingly inside her head. He didn't want an argumentative woman with opinions of her own and if she worked at it she could keep a still tongue for her sister's sake, of course she could. Posy was worth the sacrifice of a little pride.

'I have something important I want to discuss with you before we get down to the nitty-gritty of wedding arrangements,' Jude revealed. 'But I need you to agree to listen to me first without interrupting. I don't require an answer from you right now. I simply prefer to be upfront. Our relationship will be easier if we are honest with each other...'

Tansy went pink and dropped her head, that reference to honesty cutting into her. After all, she was not being truthful with him about the reality that she would come with the extra responsibility of a young child in tow. 'I can listen,' she muttered tightly.

'My original plan when I believed that I was marrying Althea was to use this marriage to father a child. Althea had agreed to that option,' Jude told her. 'And I would be delighted if you were willing to consider that possibility as well.'

Tansy was so astonished by that statement that her head swept up, stunned green eyes locking to his lean, darkly handsome features. He need not have worried about her interrupting him. She was so taken aback by that utterly unexpected confession that she could only stare in wide-eyed shock at him. A *baby*? He was actually asking her to have a *baby* with him? Was he out of his mind?

CHAPTER THREE

'Evidently I need to explain my point of view,' Jude breathed tautly as he recognised her incredulity while marvelling at how little control she had over her facial expressions. He wasn't accustomed to a woman who wore her thoughts on her face like a banner. It was educational and oddly satisfying.

'I have good reason for my aversion to marriage,' Jude contended with studious cool. 'Historically the men in my family have either made extremely poor husbands or they have married troubled women. I have no wish to follow in their footsteps and make several marriages or go through the disputes and the messy divorces that follow.' He shifted a fluid brown hand in repudiation of that depressing prospect. 'I've already lived through that pattern when I was a kid with my father and it's not for me, nor is it an ideal background against which to raise a child.'

Tansy nodded understanding of that outlook because she had checked out the Alexandris family online. Stormy separations, flagrant infidelities, divorces, custody battles and bitter feuds documented his family's shockingly volatile history in the relationship field. With those statistics behind him, it was hardly surprising that he would be especially wary of matrimony.

'But in a marriage like this, where there is no shared history or baggage, having a child could be a practical option and I am, at heart, a very practical individual. Although I have no desire to make a real marriage, I still very much need a legal heir,' Jude admitted calmly. 'It would be easiest to have one with you. I can also assure you that any child we had would be loved and cared for and that you would be richly rewarded for providing me with one.'

Tansy stared woodenly down into her coffee cup, her natural colour evaporating at his assumption that she was mercenary enough to conceive a child for a profit. It hurt to remain silent, to compress her lips on the angry defensive words ready to leap off her tongue. Calvin had forced her into a tight corner where she *had* to play a certain role. Naturally, Jude Alexandris had assumed that she was marrying him for his money, and she could not afford to tell him anything different until *after* the ceremony when Posy's future would be secure. Calvin would get his money and then he would be out of their lives, she reminded herself bracingly, thinking that at least her stepfather would never get the opportunity to use Posy the way he was using her to enrich himself.

'We would also share custody of any child. I would be amenable to most reasonable arrangements. I can give you those reassurances but naturally there is no guarantee that we could even conceive a child together,' Jude pronounced with an ironic curl to his sensual mouth. 'I don't think the male line in my family is particularly fertile, because I am an only child and so was my father.'

'Do you want my opinion on this potential plan of yours?' Tansy asked very stiffly.

'Not at this moment, no,' Jude admitted bluntly. 'For now, I only want you to mull the idea over and see if it could be a fit for you but, obviously, it's *not* a required condition for this marriage to happen.'

Some of the tension in her slight shoulders eased at that assertion and she looked back down at her coffee, forcing herself to sip it again in an effort to behave normally.

'Possibly you feel that you're too young to be tied down with the responsibility of a child,' Jude continued. 'But with my wealth, you could have nannies round the clock and becoming a mother would not deprive you of your freedom.'

Tansy almost choked on her coffee and her face burned with guilty heat because she already knew what it was like to be a young mother and there had been neither nannies nor babysitters to take the weight of responsibility off her shoulders. But, of course, she wasn't able to share that truth with him yet.

'You're keen on this idea,' Tansy said stiffly instead. 'Why? I mean, you don't even know me—'

'I don't need to,' Jude intoned confidently. 'In fact, I think it would be an advantage that we are strangers. Having a child would be a project rather than a burning mission. Emotions wouldn't be involved, and we have no past history or romantic expectations to complicate our relationship. Both of us already know that the marriage will end in divorce. I see innumerable benefits to such a detached arrangement and such arrangements are not uncommon in today's world. Friends sometimes have children together.'

Tansy's head nodded with obedient marionette stiffness. He was insane, she reflected ruefully, and as emotionally aware as a big dumb rock. He honestly believed it was possible for them to marry, have a sexual relationship and conceive a child together without anyone's emotions getting involved! What planet had he grown up on? What sort of women was he accustomed to dealing with? Had no woman ever told him that there were good reasons why human beings weren't supposed to carelessly mate like animals to reproduce? She drew in a slow, deep, self-soothing breath and remained studiously silent.

Seemingly released from tension after having broached the topic of having a child, Jude poured himself a black coffee and strode away from the table again, a tall, lithe silhouette suddenly revealed and gilded as he stepped into a shard of sunshine. 'Now, we'll get down to the basic stuff we have to organise.'

'I'm sure *I* will not be organising anything,' Tansy volunteered deadpan. 'I believe that's your department.'

Suspicious dark eyes struck hers at unnerving speed and Tansy flushed and went back to surveying her coffee again, censuring herself for having let that sarcastic comment escape, particularly when she had been doing so well at keeping quiet. Jude sank down casually on the arm of the sofa opposite her, innately graceful in his every movement. He was too close now for her to relax because her attention continually wandered back to his stunningly handsome face, tracing the sharp high cheekbones, the strong black brows framing his deep-set eyes and the lush, sensual lips that softened those arrogantly masculine features and somehow made her own tingle. When he looked directly at her, her breath caught in her throat, her heart hammered and her mouth ran dry. She shifted uneasily in her seat, alarmed by the sheer strength of his sexual attraction.

'You're quite correct. I do have everything

in hand,' Jude confessed. 'Althea has even given us our cover story but I'm afraid it has put a price on your head with the paparazzi.'

'Cover story?' Tansy repeated blankly, still struggling to pull free of the dreamy sensual spell he could plunge her into with a mere lingering glance.

'Althea and I were supposed to be getting married next week. Now I'll be marrying you instead,' Jude extended a dry explanation. 'The press and the general public will assume that I ditched her for you, which will make us look more realistic to my family since that is exactly what my father did in order to marry my mother thirty odd years ago. He was engaged to a very respectable Greek girl when he ran off with my mother.'

'Charming…so I'll be posing as the sort of woman who has no objection to carrying on with another woman's man,' Tansy commented curtly.

Jude shrugged a wide shoulder in an infuriatingly careless motion. 'Does it matter? Once Althea backed out, it was never likely to be plain sailing for us as a couple because Althea was the perfect bride as far as my relatives were concerned. *Any* other bride would be a controversial choice, so don't take that angle personally. I don't give a damn what anybody thinks, nor do you need to. All you have to do is get through the wedding reception and then we're pretty much done with family ties and socialising.'

Tansy nodded with a sinking heart, resisting the urge to say that that sounded very cold to her. But family wasn't always perfect. Didn't she know that herself? With a mother with whom, sadly, she had barely had a thought in common and a stepfather she had actively disliked? She had no excuse to feel superior, but she wasn't looking forward either to being a target of dislike and disapproval with his relations when she hadn't actually committed the sin for which she would be judged.

'The wedding will take place next week in Greece.'

'Greece?' Tansy gasped in shock, prompted into jerking forward in her seat and setting down her coffee to gape at him. 'We have to get married abroad?'

'I was born there. It's not "abroad" to me,' Jude fielded very drily.

In a frantic state of mind, Tansy wondered

how on earth she would get Posy a passport in time and, indeed, whether her stepfather would be willing to travel out to Greece with his daughter. Complications she hadn't expected were suddenly piling up around her, throwing her naive plans and expectations into crisis.

'Couldn't we just get married here?' she prompted hopefully. 'In a register office or something?'

'But that would mean that you could miss out on all the bridal pomp and ceremony—a choice which would make you a very unusual woman,' Jude remarked, subjecting her to a considering appraisal as if her suggestion were distinctly unusual and unfeminine. 'It would also greatly disappoint my grandfather who is, I'm certain, looking forward immensely to his leading role as host and master of ceremonies…'

'I'm not much for pomp and ceremony,' Tansy confided unevenly, still anxiously concerned about how she could possibly fit a ten-month-old baby into such elaborate arrangements.

Jude lifted his chin, a sudden, breathtakingly charismatic smile flashing his shapely, wilful mouth as he sprang upright without warning, that buzzing energy of his pronounced again. His smile turned the beauty of his eyes to pure glittering gold enticement. 'Yes, I'll do it!' he proclaimed, utterly disconcerting her. 'Disappointing my grandfather, Isidore, would come very naturally to me at the moment and us arriving already married will annoy the hell out of the old man. I'll arrange a register office wedding here before we fly out, but courtesy demands that we'll still have to go through the motions in Greece and suffer through a church ceremony and a party.'

Tansy nodded slowly, barely able to credit that she had succeeded in changing his mind about something, but relief was already overpowering her in a wave. At least, if he married her in London, she would be able to immediately gain custody of her little sister and she would not need to ask Calvin to put himself or his girlfriend to any extraordinary inconvenience.

'Where will we be living?' she pressed, belatedly forced to consider such facts on the back of the sudden realisation that her whole life was about to undergo a radical change.

Jude's brow pleated. 'I move between properties, as and when suits. Nothing's set in stone, but much of the time we'll be "abroad", as you call it.'

Tansy lost colour, knowing she would have to get a passport for her sister as quickly as possible, realising that out of ignorance she had totally underestimated the practicalities of life with an Alexandris. A guy as rich as Jude owned more than one home and travelled whenever and wherever he wanted, probably in a private jet. The routine restrictions that limited the choices and movements of ordinary people were unknown to him.

'You'll need a wedding gown and a new wardrobe. I have a stylist waiting next door to take your measurements,' Jude volunteered, startling her once again with that announcement. 'You will be provided with appropriate clothing to wear.'

'Provided? But—'

'Don't quibble about the unimportant details, Tansy,' Jude urged silkily. 'It's all part of the same deal and you're being paid to take on this role.'

No, *Calvin* was being paid, Tansy reflected angrily, compressing her lips on an outburst, keeping Posy's welfare first and foremost in her mind every time Jude said something that set her teeth on edge. Future husband might be an absolute dream of a fantasy man to look at, but actually living with him struck her as likely to provide a much tougher challenge. It didn't matter where or how she married him or what she wore in that temporary fake life, she reminded herself firmly. In that field Jude was undeniably right: those were insignificant details.

'I'm also hoping to keep a lid on your identity until after the wedding,' Jude informed her. 'I don't like the paparazzi. Don't talk to anyone about this marriage…and I mean, *anyone*. From you I will expect total discretion with regard to every aspect of my private life and family.'

Gripped by the warning onslaught of those piercing dark eyes set hard as granite, Tansy swallowed with difficulty. 'Yes, of course. You've got it.'

Jude wore doubt on his lean, darkly handsome features. 'I'm well aware that a lot of women like to see themselves in print but, unless it's a fashion shoot, you won't be seeing yourself in print and you won't be giving any interviews, either before or after our marriage. Is that clear?' Jude intoned.

'Crystal clear,' Tansy parried stiffly. 'Any other rules?'

'Don't tell me any lies. If you make a mistake, *own* it and tell me about it. I despise liars,' he admitted with a ringing authority that chilled her to the bone. 'The stylist is waiting for you through that door...'

Tansy rose unsteadily and moved forward, involuntarily intrigued by a man capable of arranging so much without input from anyone else. He had a strong eye for detail, she acknowledged, a knack for grasping potential problems in advance, even the little ones like what his fake wife might wear. *And he hated liars.* Her conscience twanged as she acknowledged guiltily that even he could not be expected to have guessed about the existence of a baby girl whom nobody had dared to mention. 'How did you know what time I'd be arriving to arrange a stylist?'

'I didn't.' Jude shot her an amused look. 'For the kind of money I'm prepared to spend the woman was willing to practise patience and wait until you showed up.'

As Tansy drew level with him to head towards the door he had indicated, he caught her hand in one of his to bring her to a halt. 'Let the stylist be your guide. I don't want a bride who dresses like a teenager.'

Shaken to find herself that close to him and in actual physical contact with the warmth of his big hand engulfing hers, Tansy gazed up uneasily into tawny gold eyes that were as primal to her in that moment as a lion's tracking prey. 'I only look like a teenager because I'm so skinny,' she muttered awkwardly. 'I just never rounded out like my friends. I kept on waiting for it to happen but…it *didn't*…'

As Tansy heard those unnecessarily frank words fall from her lips scarlet heat rushed into her cheeks and she wanted to bite her tongue off. But there it was: she was indisputably tiny in the places women were supposed to be curvy and feminine, more boyish than lush in shape. On the plus side she could eat whatever she liked and burn it off again without much effort, but she had always longed for the curves she lacked.

'You're not skinny, you're…slender,' Jude contradicted soft and low, something in that dark purring drawl sending a tide of awareness currenting through her from head to toe.

'Some men prefer that. Personally, I put a higher value on a more natural appearance.'

'So you say,' Tansy breathed, unimpressed by that claim, which she had heard before and found not to be true. 'But it's my bet that you wouldn't be too impressed if you got treated to natural *all* the time. Men always think they don't like make-up on a woman but I'm not sure that's the case.'

'You do have opinions,' Jude noted.

'Didn't think you wanted to hear them.'

'I do and I don't,' Jude confided. 'I prefer to keep this relationship impersonal.'

Tickled by that unlikely possibility and the sheer ignorance of human interaction with which he made that admission, Tansy shot him an amused glance. 'Well, you *will* have to work very, very hard at making sure that you don't fall madly in love with me because, I'm telling you now, you're not my type,' she heard herself tease.

Jude gazed down in visible surprise at those clear almond-shaped green eyes sparkling with laughter and the pulse at his groin kicked up a storm of interest, disconcerting him. He rested a hand down on her slight shoulder, wondering what sort of sexual chemistry it was that felled him where he stood with a totally ordinary young woman. Gold-digger, he reminded himself darkly, but inexplicably it didn't quell the desire and, with a sudden fierce impatience new to his experience, he stopped holding back and he bent his arrogant dark head and kissed her.

Tansy hadn't been prepared for that move. Later she thought that she should have been, when they were standing so close and alone and supposedly on the brink of what he *in his insanity* saw as a normal marriage. But the sensual, seeking brush of his mouth over hers made her stop breathing and freeze in astonishment. For a split second, he owned her with that kiss, *owned* her as no other man ever had because it was so exciting. Sensation burst low in her tummy and stabbed an arrow of heat down into her throbbing core. She pressed her thighs tightly together, struggling to kill that surge of awareness. And that fast, she was drinking in the unfamiliar but ridiculously arousing scent of him, discovering that that was an added aphrodisiac. He smelled good enough to eat, she found herself thinking as his arms came around her and her knees wobbled, and that all-pervasive heat spread like a traitor up through her entire body. Her hands closed on to his sleeves to steady herself.

She felt alive and blazing with energy in a way she never had before and his lips were parting hers and hers were still clinging to his, her slight frame jerking in a shocking spasm of electrified pleasure as his tongue pierced the sensitive interior of her mouth. It was like a burning torch bursting into flame inside her and every skin cell was urging her to get closer to him. Her head swam with the dizzy intensity of it, every thought overpowered by physical reaction.

Fully aroused and tense, Jude set Tansy back from him and dealt her a sizzling smile of appreciation. 'Getting to know you better promises to be especially entertaining,' he quipped as he tugged open the door that led into the room beyond.

Not if I can help it, Tansy thought, gritting her teeth, torn between wanting to slap him and slap herself for succumbing to him like a dizzy, never-been-kissed adolescent. For goodness's sake, she had literally been clinging to him! Her colour was high as the stylist approached her with a tape measure and the door behind her closed again. There was no time then for her to agonise.

The other woman was hugely efficient, questioning her about colours and styles, likes and dislikes, while bringing up outfits on her laptop for Tansy to scrutinise. Tansy, who hadn't had new clothes in longer than she remembered, found it a startling experience and when her companion moved on to asking her to preview wedding gowns on screen, it felt even more unreal to her. She was measured for every possible garment from the skin out and assured, when she tried to argue, that Mr Alexandris had specified that she was to have 'everything'. And everything in Jude's parlance seemed to encompass more clothing options than Tansy could ever have dreamt of owning and hinted at a lifestyle she had only glimpsed in her mother's favourite glossy fashion magazines.

She was on the way home again when Jude texted her the date and time for the register office wedding. It was only three days away and her eyes widened because even though Calvin had warned her that Jude was on a tight timeline, she had still underestimated the speed at which events would unfold and her life would change. But so would Posy's, she reminded herself more cheerfully. She would be able to buy new clothes and toys for her sister. There would be no more scrabbling round charity shops for garments and playthings that some other child had outgrown. With hindsight she could see that her stepfather's financial problems should have been obvious to her sooner, but then Calvin had always been very stingy about spending money on anything that did not directly benefit him.

The next day, Calvin informed her that his boss was coming out personally to the house with the prenuptial contract for her to sign. 'He's going to be very curious about how Alexandris got to know you. Just act mysterious,' he advised her.

Tansy was not required to act anything because Calvin's boss was scrupulously businesslike and polite, and he asked her no awkward questions. He even advised her to take the document to her own legal representative for a consultation. Tansy demurred and, after glancing through several pages, her brain staggered by the huge sums of money being offered to her as a mere 'allowance', insisted on signing then and there. After all, she didn't have time to waste either, not if her stepfather were to feel secure enough to sign over custody of his daughter to her.

She was not, however, that surprised when Calvin came through the front door in a rage that evening, slamming into his home study and, when he saw her in the doorway, throwing her a furious look. 'I've been made redundant by the firm…overstaffed, according to the big boss. Load of rubbish! They've worked out that I must have lined you up with Alexandris and they see it as a breach of client confidentiality!' he framed bitterly.

Tansy said nothing. Indeed, she found herself thinking that, for once, smooth, smug Calvin had got his fingers deservedly burned for his manipulative ways, but ultimately he would be richly rewarded for the marriage he had made in her name, so the punishment of losing his job wasn't that great. And *that* stung, that he could use Posy as a bargaining tool to satisfy his own greed and still have the nerve to pretend that he cared about his daughter.

The following afternoon Jude phoned Tansy.

'I've received a warning that the paparazzi

may be on the brink of identifying you,' Jude offered flatly. 'To protect you, I need to remove you from that address. No newspaper will publish your name without a photograph at the very least. A car will pick you up in thirty minutes.'

'A car? In thirty *minutes*?' Tansy repeated, nervous perspiration beading her upper lip at the prospect of her situation and potentially the reference to her baby sister being published in a newspaper. 'To pick me up and take me where?'

'A hotel, where you will remain undetected and safe until we meet at the register office tomorrow—'

'I *can't* move into a hotel!' Tansy exclaimed, worrying about Posy.

'You will accompany my security team to the hotel. I don't want you exposed by the press before my family even meet you. You don't have a choice about this,' Jude informed her grittily, and that was the end of the call.

'Jude thinks the press may be on to me,' Tansy told Calvin as she hurried downstairs and her stepfather appeared in the lounge doorway. 'He wants to have me picked up and moved to a hotel until the ceremony but I can't just walk out on Posy.'

'Of course, you can. Susie's on her way over,' Calvin told her in impatient disagreement. 'I've already warned you, Tansy. What Alexandris wants, he has to get because he could still walk away. You're not dealing with Mr Average or Mr Obliging here.'

'You could hire a nanny for Posy until tomorrow. You're about to come into money. You can afford to hire someone,' his stepdaughter reminded him doggedly. 'Then I wouldn't have to worry about her.'

'You make such a fuss about her. The kid will be *fine* with Susie. Good grief, I can't wait until you move out of here!' the blond man admitted in a burst of unhidden irritation. 'You're one of those women who always thinks they know best about everything. Alexandris is welcome to you!'

Tansy concentrated on packing an overnight bag. That she was getting married to Jude the next day felt surreal. None of the new clothing she had been promised had arrived as yet and she still only had her green dress to wear. Of course, he wasn't expecting her to appear in a wedding gown at the register office. The bridal finery would be reserved for Greece and the first day of her official wife role. She bustled next door into Posy's room where the baby was napping, and she crept about filling a bag with the baby necessities she would require for her sister's benefit the following day and set the bag aside.

Downstairs she tackled her stepfather about a topic that had begun to worry her. 'You haven't asked me to sign anything yet to take charge of Posy,' she reminded him nervously.

'It's not that simple…' Calvin frowned at her. 'Social services would insist on being involved in any change of child guardianship. The only way you can legally *have* Posy is to adopt her, but you're getting married and because of that Alexandris would have to be part of the adoption application. I suggest you take it up with him after the ceremony.'

'Adoption?' she questioned in complete bewilderment. 'But you *told* me you could *sign* Posy over to me.'

'Alterations in child custody arrangements are more formal than that and hedged around by legal safeguards,' Calvin informed her loftily. 'I can give you permission to take her abroad and I've pulled every string in the Alexandris armoury to get the kid her passport in time without Alexandris realising that it's the kid and not you who needs the passport. But I'm afraid that's the best I can do for now.'

'That's not fair, Calvin. That's not what we agreed,' Tansy protested in consternation.

At that point, her mobile rang again, and a man called Spiros, as mentioned and named by Jude, informed her that he was waiting for her at the back entrance to the house. Regretfully appreciating that she couldn't just tuck Posy into a case and pack her as well, Tansy grabbed her overnight bag and warned Calvin that Posy would need to be accompanied by her baby bag and her stroller when Tansy took charge of her the next day.

'I'll drop her off with you after the ceremony. I'll be outside the register office,' he promised cheerfully.

Tansy gritted her teeth because she didn't trust him. He had already grossly deceived her by promising to sign over custody of Posy when, as a lawyer, he must have known from the outset that that wasn't legally possible without the involvement of the local authorities. How could she have been so stupid as to trust Calvin's word about anything? On the other hand, as long as Posy seemed to be only a burden in her father's eyes, it was unlikely that he would want to reclaim his daughter in the future, Tansy reasoned, striving to silence the anxious insecurities pulling at her.

She compressed her lips as she emerged from the house. Her bag was immediately claimed by an older man in a suit, who directed her towards the narrow rear gate beyond which a car was parked in readiness.

The city hotel was famous and exclusive. Tansy felt like a fish out of water from the moment she walked through the lofty-ceilinged foyer with its marble floor and magnificent glittering crystal chandeliers. The opulent formality of her surroundings was overwhelming. She was wafted up in a lift and shown into a superb suite that included a spacious living area as well. In the bedroom she found a small selection of the garments she had chosen with the stylist awaiting her, and relief filled her because a smart outfit had been included and she thought the dress and toning jacket would be perfect for the civil ceremony. After carefully trying the clothing on, she sat in the silky robe that had been included with the gorgeous lingerie and wondered how to fill what remained of the day.

It had been so long since she had had time to herself because, for months, every day had revolved round her baby sister's feeding and sleeping schedule. She walked through her ridiculously luxurious accommodation and smiled with rueful appreciation, curling up on a sumptuous sofa to watch TV before calling room service to order an evening meal. Replete from those treats, she ran herself a bubble bath and lay in it, fretting about whether or not Susie had remembered to put Posy to bed with her favourite toy. Recalling her stepfather's accusation that she was too fussy, she wondered if that was true. Not long afterwards she climbed into the extremely comfortable bed, set her phone as an alarm and lay back, thinking in disbelief, *I'm getting married tomorrow...*

CHAPTER FOUR

TANSY ROSE INCREDIBLY early the next day and then had to fill the empty hours that stretched before the late-afternoon ceremony.

Only after lunch did she begin getting ready. She slid into the diaphanous lingerie, relishing the smooth, unfamiliar slide of silk against her skin and the pretty adornments of lace and ribbon. The dress zipped, she slipped on the high-heeled courts and donned the jacket. The unruly tumble of her hair round her shoulders made her wince because it looked untidy. Her hair needed to go up to set off the stylish rose-coloured suit. With deft fingers she braided her hair and anchored it to her head. A text arrived to tell her when she would be picked up and she was down in the foyer ahead of time, nervous as a cat on hot coals.

It isn't every day you get married, she

soothed herself, but it wasn't as if it were a real marriage. Love didn't come into their agreement and she had to admit that that made her sad, because she had always assumed that when she got married she would genuinely care about her partner. This marriage is for Posy though, she reminded herself, don't make it personal. But the recollection of her little sister frightened her as well at that moment because she was imagining how Jude Alexandris might react to the revelation that she had been less than honest with him. He would be angry. She hadn't told him an actual lie, but she certainly hadn't matched his forthrightness either.

Pale and taut, Tansy entered the waiting room in the register office feeling slightly nauseous with nerves. Jude was already there, tall, dark and devastatingly spectacular in a dark grey designer suit that accentuated his sleek, athletic build. Just looking at him stole the breath from her lungs. From the bronzed glow of his skin to his glossy black curls and wide, sensual mouth, he emanated compelling masculine allure. Her tummy flipped and her heart thumped in her ears as she collided with glittering dark golden eyes enhanced by inky black lashes. All of a sudden her legs felt disconnected from the rest of her. A hint of a smile curved his beautifully shaped mouth, lighting up his lean, shockingly handsome features, and she blinked, utterly dazzled by that sudden flash of powerful charisma.

'Who will be acting as the witnesses?' she whispered as she drew level with him.

'My security guards. These past weeks I've seen enough of lawyers to last me a lifetime,' Jude confided with grim amusement, a big hand curving to her spine to urge her forward as the registrar's assistant signalled them.

He didn't like her hair up, Jude mused, but she did look very stylish and rather more mature, although when her eyes danced with amusement, her inner teenager shone out like a neon light. He suspected she was the sort of woman given to giggling at inappropriate moments. But that sassy smile, accompanied by the downward-cast eyes and the soft flutter of her lashes as she nibbled at her fuller lower lip, ensnared his attention every time. That hint of uncertainty and shyness was incredibly enticing. He invariably went for bolder women, who laid out sex like an all-you-can-eat buffet, no questions asked, nothing on the forbidden list. He liked straightforward, he liked simple, he didn't like room left for misunderstandings or women who played games, available one day, strategically unavailable the next.

Tense at the awareness that matrimony was a solemn event and shaken by the knowledge that she was, in many ways, making a mockery of it, Tansy bolted her knees together and stood as straight and still as she could. Without fanfare the ceremony began. Jude lifted her hand and slid a fine-plaited platinum wedding band onto her finger. Her hand trembled damply in his, her responses breathless as her apprehension climbed. No matter how hard she tried to stay in the moment, her brain kept jumping ahead to Jude's likely reaction when she collected Posy from her stepfather, and she was soon right on the edge of panic. My goodness, Calvin had better be outside waiting on time, she reflected anxiously!

'So, now I'm a married man,' Jude mused reflectively as Tansy roamed ahead of him, impatient to leave the building. 'We're not in a hurry. We've plenty of time to get to the airport.'

'We're going straight to the airport?' Tansy checked in apparent surprise.

'Didn't I tell you that?'

'No,' she said flatly, because she had already noticed that he didn't bother telling her anything that he didn't think she needed to know.

'Our Greek wedding is tomorrow.'

'Oh, joy,' she muttered tautly as she stepped out onto the street, several other men joining the pair that accompanied them and fanning out across the pavement while a limousine nudged in at the kerb ahead of them.

But Tansy shifted sideways, her attention locked not to the car but to the pretty young blonde holding a baby several feet away. 'Susie...' she framed in relief, reaching for her sister and anchoring the smiling baby on her slim hip. 'Where's her stuff?'

'What stuff?' Susie asked blankly, already backing away. 'Look, I have to go. Calvin will go spare if he gets a ticket—'

'I packed a bag for her... I need her push-chair!' Tansy gasped.

Susie shrugged. 'Sorry... I didn't see it. We only brought her.'

Tansy watched incredulously as her stepfather's girlfriend hurried off without a care in the world, indeed, probably glad to see the back of both of them. Tansy out of the house and Susie freed of the expectation that she would ever have to look after Calvin's daughter again could only be a win-win on Susie's terms.

'What's going on?' Jude demanded with a frown of bewilderment, watching the baby cling to Tansy like a little limpet and dab playful little kisses across Tansy's face in what was obviously a regular game between them. Mother and child? Jude froze, shattered by the suspicion.

'Sir...?' Spiros prompted, standing at the open passenger door of the limo in readiness for their departure.

Jude unfroze with difficulty and pressed a hand to Tansy's spine to move her towards the car. With a presence of mind that astonished Jude, Spiros leant into the car and popped out a built-in child's car seat in readiness for the unexpected passenger. Jude hadn't even realised the limo offered such an option.

The woman who had told him that she was a virgin was a *mother*? And she had deliberately concealed the fact? Jude was in shock.

But he *had* married a woman who was a stranger. All he knew about her was that she liked money enough to sell herself into marriage for it. He had taken a huge risk, hadn't he? He should have had Tansy fully investigated in advance instead of simply taking her at face value. What madness had possessed him? The simple fact that the minute he had laid eyes on her he had wanted to lay her down on the nearest bed and lose himself in her? Yet when he knew so little about her, she could never have been the safe option her stepfather had sworn she was.

It was his own fault: he hadn't been willing to spare the time it would have taken to run the usual checks on Tansy. He had been in too much of a hurry, too eager to press ahead with the marriage after Althea had let him down. And his impatience had brought its own punishment.

In the ghastly silence that stretched inside the limousine, Tansy, having secured Posy in the car seat, broke out in nervous perspiration. 'I'm really, *really* sorry that I didn't tell you about her beforehand,' she whispered guiltily. 'I was scared you would change your mind about marrying me.'

Jude shot glittering dark golden eyes to her corner of the limousine and flung her a sardonic appraisal. 'You think?'

'I'll grovel if you want me to but please don't shout in front of Posy. I don't want her to get upset,' Tansy confided. 'If you're *still* taking me to Greece with you—'

'You're my wife now. I don't see that I have much choice.' Jude ground out that admission.

'I'll have to buy a load of baby things at the airport because Calvin didn't send any of her stuff with her,' Tansy muttered apologetically.

Jude knew nothing whatsoever about babies. A few of his friends had reproduced. He might be a godfather several times over but his dealings with babies were very much of the hands-off, admire-the-kid-from-a-distance nature. And then, just like that, his agile brain snapped back into gear and he dug out his phone to start handling the situation. He called his PA and told him to hire a rota of three nannies to provide the child with round-the-clock care and to ensure that the first one joined them in time for the flight out to Greece. He called his head housekeeper to order a nursery to be set up in all his homes. Those practicalities dealt with, he lounged fluidly back and simmered with pure burning rage.

The baby kept on stretching out little starfish fingers in his direction and he ignored it. It was an absurdly friendly little creature, quite impervious to the chilly atmosphere and the silence surrounding it.

He had married a single parent, a young woman with a child by an unknown man. And it would be a waste of time to set a private investigation agency on to Tansy now because within the week the international press would have exposed every single secret she had, including the identity of her child's father. Jude was rigid with anger, enraged by her brazen dishonesty from the outset of their acquaintance.

Had he known the truth about her, he wouldn't even have considered her, he reasoned angrily. He did not need nor want the hassle and inconvenience of a very young child in his life! He had nothing against children. *Thee mou*…did he not want one of his own to silence for ever Isidore's lectures about family bloodlines, duty and loyalty? But having his own child, and curbing his freedom to meet the needs of that child, was a far different prospect from the situation that Tansy had landed him into without his agreement! Unaccustomed to anything but his own will restricting him, Jude fiercely guarded his ability to do as he pleased when and where he pleased.

They arrived at the airport. Tansy bundled the kid into her arms like an unwieldy parcel and struggled to keep up with Jude as he headed for the peace of the VIP departure lounge.

By the time they arrived there, Tansy was a hot perspiring mess because Posy was a solid little girl and Tansy wasn't accustomed to carrying her for so long. After a moment of hesitation, she settled her down on the carpet at Jude's feet. 'Look, I have to go and buy essentials for Posy and she's too heavy to carry. Can you just keep an eye on her for ten minutes?' she almost whispered, her face flaming at her nerve in even asking. 'I'm sorry, I don't even have a pushchair to put her in.'

'What do I do if she starts crying?' Jude asked drily, ignoring the sudden grin that spread across Spiros's usually expressionless face.

'Lift her?' Tansy gave him a pleading look. 'She's very friendly.'

Raising her rump, the very friendly baby crawled under a chair and got stuck there. She set up a hullabaloo of complaint until Jude lifted the chair away and freed her from her self-imposed cage. By then Tansy and two of his security team had departed. Not a fast learner, Posy crawled beneath another chair and ducked her head away before whipping it back and looking expectantly at Jude with huge blue eyes. She was trying to play peekaboo without anything to hide behind, Jude registered, blanking her while a woman nearby obliged and the baby shook and wriggled with delighted laughter at the response, tousled blonde curls bouncing.

It was probably the cutest baby that Jude had ever seen, but then he didn't look at many babies and he could well be mistaken. That cuteness factor did not diminish his rage and disbelief one jot. He was appalled by the extent of Tansy's deception.

Tansy was disconcerted by the amount she had to buy merely to get Posy through a couple of days. Nappies, wipes, powdered milk, bottles, cereal, bibs, dummies, changes of clothes, a toddler cup, a couple of basic toys. A bigger embarrassment was reaching the till and realising she did not have enough in her bank account to cover such a spending spree and then Spiros startled her by stepping in with a black credit card and taking care of the payment for her. She went weak with relief. They arrived back in the VIP lounge festooned with bags of supplies. Tansy was hot and bothered and her feet were in agony from the tightness of her new shoes. She was taken aback to see a strange young brunette down on her knees on the floor entertaining Posy.

'Who's that?' she asked.

'Our new nanny. Her name's Kerry, pleasant girl, enjoys travel,' Jude advanced coolly.

'How on earth did you acquire a nanny before we've even left the airport?' Tansy whispered in disbelief.

'She's emergency cover from an agency. I have very efficient staff.'

'Posy doesn't need a nanny, and this is *not* an emergency.'

'How are you planning to get through the wedding tomorrow without a nanny?' Jude asked drily.

Tansy stiffened because she hadn't thought

ahead to that challenge and her shoulders slumped as she recognised her oversight. 'I'm really sorry about all this.'

'Not one half as sorry as I am to discover that I've married a liar and a fraud,' Jude imparted with a soft chilling bite that cut into her tender skin like the slash of a knife blade.

Momentarily tears stung the backs of her eyes and she twisted her head away to hide that weakness. She wanted to defend herself, but it was neither the time nor the place. Instead she moved forward to introduce herself to the nanny and scooped up her sister to give her a cuddle. A liar and a fraud, she thought, wincing from the description until she reminded herself impatiently that, having secured Posy's future with their marriage, she was now paying the price for her deceit.

The private jet was a great deal larger than she had naively expected. The stewardess led the way to one of a set of sleeping compartments at the rear of the plane, which was already set up with a crib for Posy.

'She's such a happy baby!' Kerry remarked cheerfully of her new charge. 'Is she always like this?'

'Pretty much and she sleeps like a log too,'

Tansy confirmed with pride as she finished changing her sister and slotted her into fresh clothing, a tight knot of tension forming in her stomach as she contemplated having to face the showdown with Jude. Time to pay the piper, she told herself ruefully, because she had neither an escape hatch nor an adequate excuse for what she had done.

She walked back to the spacious living area with its groups of opulent cream leather seats and tables. A stewardess was already serving Jude with a drink and Tansy asked for a white wine, feeling she needed something to stiffen her backbone. Her anxious gaze settled on Jude's hard classic profile. From the slash of his black brows, the angle of his strong nose and the corner of his lush shapely mouth, he was compellingly male and absolutely gorgeous, especially with the shadow of darkening stubble emphasising the sculpted hardness of his jawline.

'I know you must think very badly of me for not telling you about Posy,' Tansy said as soon as they were alone.

Jude averted his attention from the shapely length of her legs, cursing his male susceptibility for distracting him. He dealt her a lacerating glance in punishment. 'Don't fake regret with me. Why didn't you tell me that you had a baby?'

'I couldn't risk it. You might have changed your mind about marrying me,' she admitted honestly.

'*Thee mou...* I don't need any explanation for your motives!' Jude derided.

Tansy lifted her chin, a hint of challenge in her bright gaze. 'Well, actually you *do*. I didn't agree to marry you for the reasons you probably think I did.'

'I'm pretty certain that your reasons are no more complex than the size of my bank balance and the money I was willing to offer,' Jude pronounced with sardonic bite.

A wave of angry pink ran up Tansy's throat over her cheeks and up to her brow. Deeply insulted that he had dared to call her a gold-digger to her face, she gritted her teeth and settled herself down in a comfortable seat to have her drink. In an effort to fake a relaxation she was far from feeling, she kicked off the shoes that were pinching her poor toes black and blue and slid off her jacket because she was too warm. 'Well, since you already know everything there is to know about me, there's no reason for me to keep talking, is there?'

Jude surveyed her with a daunting air of incredulous hauteur, his spectacular dark golden eyes gleaming with irate warning. Tansy hitched her chin even higher in challenge, green eyes gleaming with furious defiance and determination. 'I've said sorry but I'm *not* going to grovel any more. I did something wrong and I've acknowledged it. I will do everything I can to ensure that Posy does not interfere too much with your life but there's not much more I can offer to do.'

'Of course, she'll interfere with my life!' Jude ground out, incensed by that unexpected rebelliousness of hers and her anger. She was angry with him? How *dare* she be angry with him? What right did *she* have to be angry?

'Not if you can help it…you hired a nanny fast enough!' Tansy could not resist sniping back at him. 'And you called me a liar and I'm not!'

'How do you make that out?'

'I didn't actually tell you any lies. You didn't *ask* me if I had any dependants.'

'That was for you to tell me upfront,' Jude incised crushingly.

'You're not being fair. If you were going to be so blasted picky, you should have known what questions you needed to ask,' Tansy argued defensively. 'And if you *had* asked, I would have had to answer truthfully because, whatever you think, I'm *not* a liar.'

'I wasn't prepared for someone as inventive with the truth as you appear to be,' Jude fired back at her. 'Althea has her faults, but she didn't tell me any lies.'

Tansy flushed. 'Althea said she would marry you and then changed her mind last minute!' she reminded him shortly, needled by his reference to the other woman. 'She let you down—I haven't and don't intend to! I keep my word.'

'How do you expect me to believe that now? There's nothing straight or honest about your dealings with me,' Jude condemned with icy scorn as he set his empty tumbler down with a jarring snap. 'Bringing a young child into this changes everything!'

'Maybe so,' Tansy conceded reluctantly. 'But Posy's the only secret I have.'

'Yet you even chose to pretend that you were still a virgin...*why*? Did you somehow imagine that virginity made you more appealing?' Jude demanded with lacerating contempt. 'Most men prefer an experienced woman.'

And it was only then that the extent of Jude's genuine incomprehension engulfed Tansy. He now thought she had been lying when she had admitted her lack of experience. Why was she surprised that he had no idea that Posy was her sister and *not* her daughter? Understandably, he had assumed that she was Posy's mother. Why had she not immediately realised that that was what he would think? Not that the identity of Posy's mother could have much bearing on the current situation, she conceded ruefully. After all, the key issue was that Tansy had chosen to conceal Posy's existence and her intention of bringing the child with her into their fake marriage.

Pale and taut, Tansy stood up. 'I *wasn't* lying about that. Posy's my sister, not my child.'

His strong black brows drew together and he shot her a disbelieving look. 'Your...*sister*?' he scorned. 'There's twenty-odd years between you!'

'My mother was forty-seven when Posy

was born and died soon after giving birth to her,' Tansy told him tightly, her eyes shadowing at that unhappy memory. 'I've been looking after her ever since she was born. I left my course at university while Mum was pregnant because she needed help with her business and after she died, I stayed on because…' She made an awkward gesture with her hands, her lips compressing. 'Well, Posy still needed me.'

'She's your stepfather's child?' Jude prompted with a grimace. 'So, why are you looking after her?'

Tansy tensed. 'I'd prefer not to get into that. Calvin's never been my favourite person but he wasn't cruel to Posy,' Tansy stressed uncomfortably, reluctant to tell him about her stepfather's financial stake in their marriage, for she suspected that that might cause more trouble than she was equipped to handle just at that moment. 'He just wasn't interested and his girlfriend, whom he wanted to replace me with, was only willing to look after Posy to please him and didn't have any affection for her. My sister deserves better than that.'

Jude breathed in slow and deep, slightly mollified that the baby was not *her* child and that she had not lied to him on that score, but he was equally quick to recall the conversation he had had with her when he had broached the topic of her having a child with him. He tilted his arrogant dark head back, furious condemnation in his piercing gaze. 'Even when I asked you to consider having a child with me and suggested that you might not be keen on taking on the responsibility of becoming a mother at so young an age, you didn't admit the truth,' he reminded her lethally. 'Let's be frank—not even a direct question from me would have persuaded you to reveal that child's existence!'

Guilt lacerated Tansy because she remembered that same moment and that conversation very well and knew she could not excuse her silence. 'As I said earlier, I was keen for the marriage to take place. I didn't want to give you a reason to write me off as a possibility.'

'And, of course, it's too late now,' Jude completed flatly and then his eyes fired pure scorching gold with rage as he narrowed his fierce gaze on her. '*Thee mou*...no wonder you were so eager for us to marry *before* we went to Greece! That's what made it possible for you to continue concealing the child's existence from me. You were determined to have that ring safely on your finger first.'

There was no way of arguing that point and Tansy bit her lower lip and nodded grudging agreement. Jude, it seemed, had a forensic brain. He would unpick and expose every evasion and half-truth she had given him until there was nothing left for her to hide behind. She glanced up, encountering liquid golden eyes that sent a buzzing energy pulse through the most sensitive areas of her body and the sensation shook her inside out because no man had *ever* made her feel like that before. Her nipples tight buds pushing against her bra, her slender thighs trembling, the heart of her hot and damp, she hastily averted her attention from him.

The same heat pulsed through Jude like a drumbeat and he was furious with himself. The throbbing swelling at his groin was an unwelcome reminder of his lack of control around her. Although shouldn't that persistent sexual attraction be something to celebrate rather than something to regret when they were already married? He wanted the full truth of what was going on with her stepfather

and then he wanted her in his bed to ease the hard edge of frustration she induced. Whether he liked it or not, evidently they were stuck with the baby and condemned to be a family of three rather than a carefree couple. Dark fury rippled through his big, powerful frame.

'There's an imbalance here,' Jude mused. 'You've landed me with a child in my life for the next couple of years. I'm not the forgiving kind, but if you were willing to consider compensating me for your lies and omissions I may be persuaded to overlook your flaws.'

Tansy lifted clear green eyes full of incomprehension and her smooth brow pleated. 'I don't understand.'

Jude studied her with angry, calculating intensity. 'Try to give me that baby I asked you to consider having and I will not only forgive you but I will also treat your sister as though she were my own child.'

Silence fell. Tansy's eyes rounded and widened. 'Oh, my word, you're trying to use this to put pressure on me! That is so...*so* unscrupulous.'

'And you're *surprised*?' Jude sliced in very drily. 'You're dealing with an Alexandris, not an angel. I was taught to wheel and deal from childhood.'

Shock set in hard on Tansy. She could barely credit that he would use her plight and her current guilt to bargain with her and do so with such a shameless lack of remorse. But what was even worse, she discovered just then, was that softly given promise to treat Posy the same as his own child. That was *huge*, particularly when it related to a little girl who had never known a father in her short life. Tansy knew how much she had missed having a daddy and some day her sister would go through the same experience, only not if she agreed to Jude's suggestion that she try to have a child with him.

'One question,' Tansy muttered unevenly. 'If I were to agree to this, would you be willing to apply to adopt Posy with me?'

'Of course.'

Tansy felt dizzy with relief because her stepfather continued to lurk at the back of her mind as a lingering threat to his daughter's security. Removing Posy from Calvin's care without Tansy having any legal right to keep the child had worried her. Calvin had deliberately misled her by not delivering on the promise he had originally made and why was that? Only if Tansy adopted her sister could she feel that the child was safe from her father's intrigues, and with Jude by her side, Posy would then be fully protected.

'If you're willing to adopt Posy with me, I'll agree to try to have a child with you,' Tansy conceded tautly, wondering if she was crazy to lay so much of herself on the line, but then thinking about Posy and knowing she would do anything to keep that little girl safe and secure. And providing her sister with that security and possibly the joy of another sibling as well would be a good result, she told herself squarely.

A slanting smile slashed Jude's beautiful mouth and her heart skipped a beat and her mouth went dry. 'Let's have dinner, *hara mou*,' he suggested smoothly.

CHAPTER FIVE

'I'LL TAKE POSY,' Jude offered as he lifted Tansy down out of the helicopter and turned to Kerry to extend his arms.

Cross at having her night's sleep disturbed, the baby pouted and then succumbed to the invitation, a man being a new source of attraction in her mainly female world. Ensconced in Jude's arms, Posy smiled sleepily.

'That's the first time you've used her name,' Tansy remarked as she accompanied him into the waiting SUV.

'She will be family now.'

His statement felt reassuring because Tansy had yet to have anyone stand by her side when it came to guarding Posy's welfare and her fear of Calvin's potential interference receded a little. It was getting dark rapidly and Tansy peered at the formal gardens stretching ahead of them and then off into the distance at the walls she could dimly see in one direction. 'Where's your grandfather's house?' she asked.

'Over the hill. The estate is gigantic. Other people downsize at his age but Isidore *upsized*,' Jude told her wryly. 'This place used to belong to one of his biggest business rivals and he bought it the minute it came on the market. He's very vain and he likes to live like a king.'

'He sounds quite a character,' Tansy commented as the car mounted the hill and turned down a central drive to begin an approach to a huge building that, with its twin wings, resembled a French chateau and was lit up like a firework display both inside and outside. 'Wow…'

'Isidore may be terse with you,' Jude warned her. 'He expected me to marry Althea and he doesn't like surprises. He won't like you having a child in tow either and probably won't believe that she's your sister.'

'I can cope with rudeness,' Tansy said ruefully.

'You have my permission to be equally rude back. He thinks women should be seen and not heard and all three of his late wives fell into the quiet-little-mouse category.'

'Oh, dear.' Tansy grimaced, nervous perspiration dampening her upper lip as the vast dwelling ahead drew closer and the SUV pulled up at the foot of the steps.

Jude strode up the steps, Posy still safely held in his arms. The opulence of the big foyer was overpowering. Mirrors, gilded furniture and giant crystal chandeliers obscured Tansy's vision and made her blink in disorientation. Jude addressed an older woman who approached him with pronounced subservience and he handed Posy back to the nanny.

'Cora will show them to their rooms.'

'I should go up with them,' Tansy contended, the food she had eaten earlier sitting like a lead weight in her tense stomach.

Jude closed a hand over hers before she could accompany the nanny. 'No, we don't run scared in this family,' he told her firmly, urging her on with him into a room where a small portly man stood by a huge marble hearth.

'Jude!' Isidore Alexandris exclaimed in welcome, his heavily lined face smiling even while his deep dark eyes remained steady, and that was the only word Tansy understood because a flood of Greek followed.

'And this is my wife, Tansy.' Jude switched smoothly back to English as he moved her forward.

'Tansy…' The smile on the older man's face melted away and he dealt Tansy a brusque nod of acknowledgement before continuing his conversation with his grandson in Greek. He was virtually blanking her, Tansy registered, but she rather suspected that being ignored by Isidore could be more comfortable than attracting his attention. The exchange between the two men was sharp-edged and Isidore pursed his thin lips, his displeasure at Jude's replies patent but the affection in his gaze when he looked at his grandson remained, despite his irritation. While Jude might seemingly be either unaware of or indifferent to his grandfather's attachment to him, that warmth was blatantly obvious to Tansy.

Feeling like a third wheel, Tansy hovered until Jude wrapped an arm round her stiff spine and guided her back out of the room. 'Doesn't he speak English?' she whispered as they crossed the echoing foyer towards the sweeping staircase.

'Like me, he was educated at Eton,' Jude offered. 'He was being cutting.'

'Did you have an argument about me?'

'No. He will accept that you're my wife for the foreseeable future. He's not happy about it but he'll settle because he's finally got me married off,' Jude breathed sardonically.

'Have you been that hard to get to the altar?' Tansy teased in an excess of relief at having so swiftly escaped his intimidating grandfather.

Long powerful legs ascending the stairs, leaving her breathless in her efforts to keep up, Jude vented a humourless laugh. 'You have no idea. Marriages don't work out very well in my family. Of course, I was avoiding it.'

'Then why now?' Tansy asked curiously. 'What's changed?'

Dark golden eyes swept her face assessingly on the landing. 'We'd have to be a lot closer for me to explain my reasons.'

Tansy flushed and jerked a slight shoulder in receipt of that snub, falling silent as Jude strode through a door at the foot of a corridor, strolling confidently through a beautiful sitting room adorned with fresh flowers into an equally large bedroom.

Jude approached a pile of boxes sitting on a low table. 'Isidore is loaning you some family jewellery to wear tomorrow. Festoon yourself in diamonds. Don't worry about being vulgar or excessive. He loves to show off our wealth.'

'OK,' Tansy muttered.

'I have business to discuss with Isidore,' Jude told her, striding towards the sitting room. 'I'll see you later.'

Tansy fell still. 'We're both sleeping in here?'

Jude hitched a mocking black brow. 'We're married, and did you really expect separate rooms when the old man is desperate for me to provide the next generation of the family?'

Tansy shifted uneasily where she stood. 'You said you'd give me time.'

'And so I will,' Jude murmured lazily. 'I'm not sex-starved. I can share a bed with you and resist temptation.'

On the way out of the room, he came to a sudden halt and glanced back at her from lushly lashed narrowed eyes. 'I should warn you. Althea Lekkas will be one of the guests tomorrow. Isidore invited her and I suppose, on the face of things, it will look better from the guests' point of view that there's no apparent bad blood between us,' Jude declared with a curled lip because he was already weary of Althea's numerous texts begging for details about his replacement bride. He just wanted her to back off and leave him in peace.

'No skin off my nose,' Tansy countered brightly. 'I know nothing about her or your relationship.'

'We've known each other since we were kids. She was my first love. It didn't work out but we've remained friends,' Jude advanced with a shrug.

His *first* love. She wondered why that description only increased her curiosity. It wasn't as though she were attached to Jude in any way or possessive of him. Tansy stiffened, irritated by her desire to know more about Jude's past than she had any good reason to know. Keep it impersonal, she urged herself, keep that distance. They could be polite and civilised *and* sexual, she assured herself, without bringing any real feelings into it. It *had* to be that way; she couldn't afford to get involved on any deeper level because that way she would get hurt. Jude needed a wife and he would be happy if she gave him a child, but he had said that at most they would be together for only a couple of years. Nothing lasting or permanent was on offer and it would be a disaster if she allowed herself to become fond of him on any level.

Jude departed and Tansy investigated the other doors that led out of the bedroom, discovering a packed dressing room. Her wedding dress was there in a protective wrap and she uttered a quiet prayer that it would fit. All the other clothes that had been ordered that first day in Jude's office sat in neat piles on shelves, hung from rails and tumbled in a rainbow of opulence in drawer after drawer. Shoes and bags filled an entire cabinet. She had only ever seen such an array of clothing inside a big store.

In a haze of growing exhaustion, she left the suite to check that Posy had settled for the nanny. Unsure where her sister had been put to sleep, she had only reached the top of the stairs when the housekeeper, Cora, appeared and showed her where to go. Posy was soundly asleep in a fancy cot with Kerry in the room next door. On the way back to bed,

Cora asked Tansy if she had any special requests for breakfast the following morning while informing her that Jude's grandfather had instructed that the usual technicians attend Tansy to prepare her for her wedding day.

Tansy twirled in front of the cheval mirror, pleased with the perfect fit of the gown. An off-the-shoulder neckline and tight half sleeves completed the sophisticated look. Delicate beads and fabulous diamonds shimmered as she moved. Romantic lace motifs overlaid the tulle that snugly encased her from the shoulder, with the skirt falling in soft layers to her feet, hemmed by the same lace that swept back into a small cathedral train. Her mass of hair was up to anchor the magnificent diamond tiara that sat like a crown on her head, while the collar of diamonds encircling her throat and the matching bracelets cast rainbow reflections on the rug below her feet.

From the moment Tansy had wakened she had been waited on hand and foot. Her breakfast had been served in bed with the indent on the pillow next to hers the only evidence that at some stage of the night Jude must have joined her and slept beside her. Tansy remembered nothing after climbing into the blissfully comfortable bed. A hair stylist had arrived after breakfast, soon followed by a nail technician and a beautician. Tansy had insisted on doing her own make-up because she didn't like it too heavy. A maid arrived to tell her that Jude's grandfather, Isidore, was waiting downstairs to accompany her to the church.

Tansy descended the stairs with great care because her heels were extremely high. She was disconcerted when the older man extended an arm to her and murmured almost pleasantly, 'You look very well indeed, my dear, and the diamonds are the ultimate embellishment. Do you like them?'

'Yes… I've never worn diamonds before. Have these pieces been in the family long?'

It was a lucky question. Isidore Alexandris smiled and rested back in the limousine to tell her the history of the jewellery she wore, careful to tell her the worth of each item as well as what was paid for it at auction. She was suitably impressed. That conversation lasted them through the heavy Athens traffic all the way to the doors of the grand church chosen for the traditional ceremony. There she was surprised to see Jude in the entrance hall waiting for her, surrounded by his bodyguards.

Tansy walked through the double doors and Jude fell silent. An impossibly slender figure in delicate white draperies, she looked dazzlingly beautiful. The superb collar of diamonds encircling her elegant white throat and the tiara shining in her luxuriant dark blond hair were the perfect additions. He was stunned by the smile on his grandfather's face because it looked genuine.

'You look superb,' Jude breathed, handing her a beautiful bouquet of tumbling white roses and gypsophila.

Pleased colour brightened Tansy's cheeks as she looked up at him. Even in her high heels, he still towered over her and he looked hotter than hot in a splendidly tailored dark grey tailcoat, waistcoat and narrow trousers, his glossy black curls glinting in the sunshine illuminating the glorious stained-glass window behind him. Shimmering dark golden eyes of appreciation were welded to her and slow, pervasive heat filtered through her, making it a challenge to breathe.

'You may not have done as badly as I thought with her,' Isidore whispered, startling his grandson before he could walk down the aisle with his bride. 'She's bright and she may be penniless but so, essentially, is Althea, and Althea's flighty into the bargain, which is worse.'

Jude almost laughed, astonished that Tansy had won even that amount of grudging approval from the older man, who only the night before had sworn that no Alexandris had ever chosen a less worthy bride.

Tansy hadn't realised that the Greek Orthodox ceremony would be as long or as elaborate. The exchange of rings, the carrying of a candle followed by the symbolic crowns and the circling of bride and groom were driven by Jude's nudging guidance and she blushed and stumbled and hesitated more than once, just praying that her uncertainty went unnoticed. The church was packed. At the end of the service, her slim shoulders relaxed from rigidity and she was able to accompany Jude back outside with a little more assurance.

'I could have done with a rehearsal for that,' Tansy quipped, ready to reach for Posy when she saw her in the nanny's arms but prevented by Jude.

'You can see her at the reception,' he pointed out smoothly as a wall of cameras and shouted questions greeted them outside the church.

'When did your mother pass away?' Tansy asked curiously as they climbed into the waiting limo.

'Clio's still alive. Where did you get the idea that she was dead?' Jude demanded.

'I just assumed. I mean, I read online about the divorce and your father's car crash but that was years ago. I thought that a mother would always attend her son's wedding and there's been no sign of her—'

'Clio would sooner drink poison than come to an Alexandris social event and run into my grandfather. They hate each other.'

'That's sad,' Tansy opined. 'When you don't have much in the way of close family you'd prefer them to get on.'

'That's life,' Jude pronounced cynically but his lean, strong face had clenched hard, hinting that he was less comfortable with those divisions than he was prepared to acknowledge. 'I may not have close family but I do have numerous cousins. I saw little of my mother growing up. We're not close. She's Italian and she returned to Italy following the divorce.'

It all sounded very detached to Tansy and she wondered if that was why Jude was so hard and unemotional or if, indeed, that facade of his was simply a pretence, because she could sense that his reaction to any reference to his mother was sensitive and guarded. What was that reserve of his hiding? 'Were you close to your father?' she asked curiously.

Jude turned exasperated dark eyes on her. 'What is this? Psychology for beginners?'

'Never mind. I like knowing what makes people tick. I didn't mean to pry,' she responded lightly, stealing a glance at his unimpressed expression and then laughing out loud. 'Well, yes, I *was* being nosy but you weren't supposed to pick me up on it!'

A reluctant grin slashed his sculpted lips. 'I spend my life in business meetings interpreting body language and expressions.'

Tansy had the tact not to remind him that he hadn't contrived to read her very well and guess that she was hiding things when they first met. The wedding breakfast was being held in a pillared ballroom in the mansion. Reunited with Posy, Tansy ignored the questioning appraisals coming their way and settled in for a stint of polite socialising, eating and smiling dutifully at the many toasts. She noticed Althea Lekkas long before she realised who the other woman was and that was only after someone hailed her from across the room. The glowing glamorous blonde, her gold metallic dress melded to her shapely curves, was fizzing with energy, flirting like mad and attracting a lot of male attention.

When Jude was taking Tansy round to meet people, the same woman walked right up to them. 'Hi, I'm Althea,' she said brightly. 'May I steal the bridegroom for a little private chat?'

Keen not to seem territorial while marvelling at Althea's nerves of steel, Tansy stepped away and headed for the cloakroom to freshen up, wondering if it was too soon to get changed because they were leaving in an hour. Jude had told her so without telling her where they were going. But then, explaining himself was not Jude's strongest talent. He behaved as though he had never been a part of a couple before and was unable to make that mental shift to sharing details in advance or even discussing his plans. Or possibly that arrogance was simply part and parcel of his attitude to her, the woman he had *paid* to marry him. And maybe it was rather naive of her to believe that he should consult her about what happened in their lives.

Walking back to the ballroom, Tansy heard raised voices and recognised Jude's. Her smooth brow furrowing because he sounded both angry and frustrated, she crossed the hall to a light-filled room full of exotic plants where Althea and Jude appeared to be involved in an argument. Of course, they were conversing in Greek, so she had no idea what they were saying. The blonde appeared to be trying to soothe Jude, tugging down and clinging to his arms when he lifted them high in a gesture of seething impatience and then leaning forward to plant her full pink mouth on his in a fervent kiss. That display of intimacy, that assumption that her kisses would be welcome, was blatant as a police siren in its boldness. In response, Jude pressed the blonde back against the wall, pinning her hands to her sides, speaking to her in a low intense voice. What she was witnessing struck Tansy as the very essence of passion playing out before her appalled gaze.

Although it was the hardest thing she had ever done, Tansy snapped her spine straight, turned her head away and went upstairs to remove her wedding dress and change. Jude's relationship with his old friend and former first love was none of her business, she told herself briskly even while another, more primal voice in the back of her mind was shouting something far more aggressive. Jude was her husband and he was already cheating on her and that hurt her like a knife thudding into her chest, igniting a host of reactions she had not expected to feel. Instead of cool, critical detachment she found angry, bitter resentment and revulsion roaring through her and she shuddered with the force of her feelings. So much for all that talk of his about respecting fidelity within marriage! Possibly, though, she was a little oversensitive to the pain of being cheated on because it wasn't the first time it had happened to her. And watching the speed at which Calvin had moved on after her mother's death had only reinforced her trust issues.

At nineteen she had lost faith in her own

judgement when a spiteful girl and a lying, manipulative boyfriend had conspired to hurt and humiliate her. Egged on by her flatmate and supposed friend, Emma, Ben had tried to get her into bed with him to win a bet. In effect a price tag had been put on Tansy's virginity and that had destroyed her pride and hurt her heart because she had fancied herself in love with Ben. Emma's cruelty had inflicted another wound, particularly once Tansy had realised that Emma had been sleeping with Ben the whole time he had been dating Tansy.

Shaking free of that sordid recollection, Tansy studied Posy, snug in her cot and blissfully, innocently asleep, leaving her big sister longing to experience that same sense of peace and security. Kerry hovered in the doorway. 'We'll be joining you again tomorrow, Mrs Alexandris. Don't worry about her.'

Tansy flushed as she registered that even the nanny seemed to know their schedule and destination while Jude had chosen to leave his bride in the dark. She found two maids packing her clothes in the bedroom and scooped up cropped linen trousers and a comfortable ivory top to wear with flat sandals. She got changed in the bathroom, but she still couldn't think straight. Every time she tried to focus on something else, she would see Althea's mouth plastered to Jude's.

Why on earth had Althea cancelled the wedding if she still wanted Jude? It could have been Althea in the church today marrying Jude, Tansy reasoned painfully, and she felt like an idiot for believing him when he had said he and Althea were only friends. What sort of weird relationship did the two of them have? Perhaps they had one of those passionate on-and-off relationships that people sometimes got caught up in, a relationship full of drama and confrontation and feverish reconciliations. Yet he had married *her*, Tansy reminded herself, compressing her lips, bewilderment lacing the other fiery emotions she was experiencing.

Tansy was pacing and lost in troubling thoughts when Jude strode into the bedroom, dismissing the maids at almost the same time as he began stripping off his formal wedding attire. His lean, strong face was set in grim angles and hollows, his tension palpable.

'I saw you kissing Althea,' Tansy told him, not having planned to admit that but finding those incendiary words flying straight off her tongue.

Jude grimaced. 'That's all I need!' he bit out in a raw undertone, stripping off his boxers to stride naked into the bathroom.

Her face hot from being exposed to all that bronzed masculine nudity, Tansy was nonplussed by that lack of response. What? No apology? No explanation? Not even a thin tissue of lies aimed at staging a cover-up? She could hear the shower running full force, a cascade of water splashing down on the tiles. Only minutes later, Jude emerged again, his wet curls wildly tousled, a towel loosely wrapped round his lean hips as he stalked into the dressing room. Sheathed in what she suspected to be his favourite ripped faded jeans and a loose black shirt that was still unbuttoned, parted edges showing off a slice of broad brown muscular chest, Jude joined her again. A dark shadow of stubble framed his strong jaw line, a jaw that was set granite hard.

'We'll discuss Althea later. I've just spent thirty minutes clearing that car crash up without causing a public scene. I refuse to deal with another scene from you in my grandfa-

ther's home, where nothing is truly private,'
Jude intoned with chilling cool. 'This is *not*
your moment.'

Utterly taken aback by his brazen lack of
discomfiture, Tansy raised her head high.
'Obviously not, since even though you married me yesterday I seem to be the only person round here who doesn't know where
we're heading next!' she proclaimed heatedly.

Dark golden eyes rested on her. 'My bolt-
hole in Rhodes. It's private and on the beach.
It's also a short flight.'

'You should have answered me about Althea,' Tansy condemned, thoroughly enraged
by his self-control and his unrepentant attitude.

'We haven't got the time to get into something that complex right now,' Jude countered
drily, planting a directional big hand to her
spine. 'Come on. I can't wait to get out of
here.'

He escorted her down the stairs, where
he exchanged a few fleeting words with his
grandfather in the hall before urging her out
of the mansion and into an SUV that ran them
back down to the helipad, where the helicopter awaited their arrival.

As she boarded, sidestepping Jude's attempt to lift her, Tansy's hair blew back from her delicate features, highlighting the almost aggressive angle of her chin. Just his luck, Jude thought, he had married a gold-digger with moral principles and a surprising amount of backbone, because she had done the unexpected: she had challenged him openly.

As the helicopter took off, however, Jude compressed his wide, sensual mouth hard. He would have to tell her about his history with Althea and he was outraged by the prospect of having to explain himself to *any* woman. Sadly, circumstances were about to force him to share private stuff that he did not usually share with anyone, but it was necessary to keep Tansy on side. He *needed* a child with Tansy, and he could not afford to alienate her. Hadn't he thrown his life open to a stranger? Hadn't he married her in the hope of having a child and to protect his mentally fragile mother from a loss that might break her again? It was unthinkable to him now that he would not ultimately win his complete freedom with the sacrifices he had already made.

And yet Tansy had already *deceived* him, *lied* to him, *cheated* him of his expectations, he reminded himself fiercely. His lean brown hands clenched into fists because he was so bitterly weary of women trying to use him, trying to profit from him. Yet if she did give him a child it would be a commercial transaction like their marriage, so how was he any better than she was? He himself might have been conceived in love but even by the time he was born his mother had hated his father as much as she'd loved him.

He was an Alexandris and that was how it was for an Alexandris, he reasoned grimly. He got the money, the worldly acclaim and success, he got nothing else deeper or more meaningful from anyone...even Althea. Her love had been whisper-thin and warped. As for his troubled mother, she could barely tell the difference between her adulterous late husband and her living son, who had learned very young never, *ever* to cheat on any woman because that pain could *break* someone vulnerable...

His brilliant eyes shadowed with his most tragic memory of his mother, Clio, and he paled. Of course, he had naively believed that there might be more to Tansy before he'd married her, *before* she'd chosen to show him her true colours of lies and deceit. But she was a gold-digger, there was no denying that now, and, ironically, he was much safer with Tansy, a tough, greedy little woman who likely wouldn't care if he bled to death in front of her...

CHAPTER SIX

THE HELICOPTER LANDED in what looked like a forest glade.

Tansy jumped out, full of curiosity. 'You have a cabin in the woods?' she remarked in surprise, briefly forgetting that she wasn't actually speaking to Jude as yet. Ironically, though, the fact that he hadn't even tried to communicate with her during the flight had left her feeling ridiculously excluded.

'No, not a cabin,' Jude asserted, leading the way down a path through the pine trees, dense vegetation on all sides preventing her from catching much of a view of anything.

But the smell of the sea flared her nostrils and she saw a glint of water through the forest of tall straight trunks surrounding her. They emerged out of the shade into the evening sunshine and her eyes went wide as she saw the ancient stone walls intersected by ornamental turrets rising in front of her. 'A castle?' she whispered in disbelief.

'I saw it from the water one afternoon a few years ago. It was a medieval ruin until it was illegally developed by a rich eccentric in the nineteen twenties. It was almost derelict again by the time I bought it and fixed it up. It's the smallest property I own. I had to renovate a terrace of farmworker cottages nearby to accommodate staff.'

'I suppose it's unthinkable that you could manage for yourself,' Tansy sniped.

'I will never be able to live safely without security, nor will you. The family name does come with a downside of high risk,' Jude told her drily.

'Oh, believe me,' Tansy said tartly, 'I've already seen that for myself!'

Jude gritted his even white teeth and shot her a shimmering dark golden glance of condemnation. 'You're wrong about me, *very* wrong!'

Tansy said nothing more, accompanying him into an unexpectedly cosy hall and up a stone staircase into a spacious bedroom, made airy by contemporary furniture in spite of the natural stone walls and narrow window embrasures through which sunshine glimmered in long shards across the floor. 'A drink?' Jude prompted.

'Wine,' Tansy said flatly. 'Please...'

'Althea and I...a tangled tragic tale,' Jude murmured grittily as he opened a cupboard kitted out with a comprehensive bar and refrigerator. 'We were childhood sweethearts with the approval of both families. Isidore very much approved of the Lekkas pedigree, if not their lack of fortune. At sixteen, she was my first lover and I was hers and I adored her. My best friend, Santos, was in love with her as well but I trusted him, I trusted them both...' Jude glanced up from the beer he was pouring and saluted her with it, a cynical curve to his expressive mouth. 'You're only that young and innocent once.'

As Tansy guessed with a sinking heart where the tale seemed to be going, she tensed, suddenly feeling that she was being made aware of stuff she wasn't entitled to know, and then reddening on the memory that she had seen him in Althea's arms and that, as his wife, she *did* have a right to know their back story if it was relevant.

'I did a business degree at Harvard and one

summer I worked as an intern in New York.'
Jude poured wine and extended a glass to her.
'Althea slept with Santos while I was away. It
only happened once but there was no reasonable excuse for it and, even though I believed
her when she said it wouldn't ever happen
again, I couldn't forgive her for it.'

Her back stiff with the tension in the atmosphere, Tansy sat down in an armchair and
clutched her glass with both hands as if it
were a lifesaver. 'I can understand that.'

'But Althea has never understood or accepted it,' Jude declared flatly. 'Initially I refused to have anything to do with her. I was
very bitter. It was only after her father approached me on her behalf that I appreciated
that our friends had made her a social pariah.
That was more punishment than I felt she
should suffer, and I made an effort to toler-
ate her again.'

'What about…er…your friend Santos?'

Jude gave her a wry glance. 'I found it easier to forgive him because he genuinely loved
her. He asked her to marry him afterwards
and she said no. He was devastated. He got
drunk one night and crashed his motorbike.

I've always secretly blamed Althea for his death as well.'

Tansy sipped wine into her dry mouth in fascination because she couldn't take her eyes off his darkly handsome face while one emotion after another flickered there, teaching her that he felt much more than either he or she had been prepared to acknowledge. Just like her, he knew exactly what hurt and betrayal felt like and what it felt like when the object of your love revealed clay feet and came crashing down off a pedestal. 'What Althea did was a disaster for all three of you,' she remarked ruefully. 'So why, bearing that problematic past in mind, were you, only a few weeks ago, considering marrying her and having a child with her?'

'She offered when she found out that I was in a tight corner. Initially I said no, but I was desperate and I did think better the devil you know,' Jude admitted, startling her once again with his frankness. 'After all, it's been almost nine years since we were together and I thought it was safe. She was married to someone else for four of those years and was recently divorced. I assumed she'd moved on long ago.'

'Only she hadn't,' Tansy guessed.

'When she said she couldn't go through with the marriage she insisted she still had feelings for me, so I backed off immediately,' Jude clarified. 'That was a major turnoff for me. But today when she came to the wedding, she told me that I wasn't supposed to run off and find someone else to marry after she dropped out.'

'Why? What were you supposed to do?' Tansy pressed with bemused curiosity.

His stunning dark golden eyes shadowed, and his beautiful shapely mouth twisted with exasperation. 'Apparently, Althea had her moves all planned out. The cancellation was a power play. She thought that when she dropped out at the last minute I would panic and come back and offer her *more*.'

'More?' Tansy queried, smooth brow pleating.

'A more lasting marriage, maybe even love.' Jude winced in disquiet at the concept and sprawled fluidly down on a love seat, one denim-clad knee gracefully raised. 'But I couldn't do it. I didn't want to be with her long-term and I couldn't ever love her again because fidelity for me is an unbreakable rule.'

'Then what was that I saw between you this afternoon?' Tansy asked him baldly, wondering if any man had ever looked so spectacularly beautiful in ripped jeans and a shirt, the sheer breathtaking perfection of his sculpted face and lean, powerful physique compelling.

'Althea losing the plot at our wedding. She had taken something…she was as high as a kite and furious with me. That's when she told me she'd deliberately cancelled the wedding, expecting me to offer her a more permanent deal, and I was disgusted with her because she should have moved on from me long before now… Wouldn't any normal woman have moved on?' he prompted in a raw undertone of appeal.

Tansy nodded weakly, marvelling that Althea had betrayed him in the first place, while thinking that most women would be challenged to fully get over a guy as rich, beautiful and sexy as Jude Alexandris. It had been a fatal mistake for Jude to offer that convenient marriage, so near and yet so far from what Althea still so desperately wanted to reclaim.

'She's just had bad luck with other men,

that's why she keeps on coming back to the idea that—'

'You're the one and only who got away,' Tansy slotted in wryly. 'So, what about that kiss?'

'*She* kissed me! By then, I'd regained my temper and I was trying to get her to pull herself together and calm down. Her brother took her home. He was very apologetic. I think her family are considering putting her in rehab.' Jude grimaced and raked long brown fingers through his glossy curls in a gesture of frustration. 'I feel guilty about her. I even feel guilty for being grateful that she *did* cancel the wedding because if I had married her, it would have turned into a nightmare.'

Tansy wanted to hug him for being so honest with her and she could only be impressed by the sheer depth of feeling he had hidden so well from her. He wasn't a bad guy. He wasn't a cheat and he still had sufficient generosity and compassion to be concerned for the woman who had once cruelly betrayed his trust. 'I misunderstood. I thought I was seeing a lover's quarrel… That argument and her behaviour seemed so intimate,' she confided uncomfortably. 'And there's no way I would be sleeping with you if you were carrying on with other women at the same time! I couldn't live like that, so if you're planning on playing away, please leave me out of it.'

Jude lifted and dropped a broad shoulder. 'It's really not a big deal for me to promise you that I will not be with anybody else while we're together. Cheating is against my principles,' he confided in a driven undertone, his strong facial bones standing out stark beneath his bronzed skin. 'I grew up with a father who screwed around on my mother and I watched his affairs drive her into a nervous breakdown because she couldn't cope with his behaviour.'

'Oh…' Tansy was shocked because, while she had read about his father's womanising reputation online, she had not factored in the damage that his parents' broken relationship must also have inflicted on Jude. His compassion for his mother's suffering during her time with his father impressed her. He might not be close to the woman, might not see much of her, but he clearly still cared deeply about her.

'I'm probably the last man alive who would cheat on you,' Jude quipped with grim amusement, setting down his glass and opening his arms. 'Now come here… I want to…*finally*… kiss my bride.'

Tansy stood up, uncertainty stamped in every line of her bearing. Jude dropped his legs down and eased her closer to stand between his spread thighs.

He plucked at the waistband of her cropped trousers. 'Is it possible to lose the trousers? I prefer skirts.'

'Trousers are more practical for travelling.'

'You've got me now, and first-class travel. You don't ever need to be practical again,' Jude intoned, flipping loose the button at her waist slowly enough to allow her time to back away if she wanted to.

Only, Tansy discovered, she *didn't* want to because she was much more invested in wondering what Jude would do next. His action released a heady mix of terror and longing inside her. The relief of his explanation about Althea, the sudden loss of her every excuse to stay distant from him, had left her dizzy, unsure and confused. And then there was the warmth he had evoked while he spoke, the emotion he so rarely showed but so definitely felt, the pain he had exposed. All of a sudden, gorgeous, sexy, intimidating Jude was a human being, who had been wounded just as she had been by betrayal, and he no longer felt like a potentially threatening stranger she had to be on her guard with.

He ran down the zip and the trousers fell round her ankles. He lifted her out of them and held her stationary, smoothing appreciative hands down over slender hips covered by the thin band of the lace thong she wore, trailing long, lazy fingers over the long length of her shapely legs, sweeping them up again to briefly encircle her tiny waist before stroking up over her narrow ribcage. *'Like,'* he stressed without embarrassment. 'Beautiful, utterly perfect…'

Tansy could barely believe what he was saying. Colour lanced her cheeks as he lifted her and tipped her forward so that she straddled his lap, the denim of his jeans rubbing against her knees as she splayed her legs, so self-conscious now that she felt as though a burning torch were flaring up inside her. He framed her face with his big hands and captured her parted lips with his and it was as if an adrenalin rush engulfed her, his tongue darting into her mouth as subtle as a sword and then plunging deep, and her head spun while the edge of his teeth plucked at her full lower lip. And that fast she was on fire, rocking back from him, feeling her shirt drift down her arms as his palms grazed over her bra-clad breasts until the bra too was gone and he was toying with her achingly sensitive nipples, making her gasp into his mouth and struggle for breath. Liquid flame ran to the heart of her and pooled there even as his hands slid down to her hips and ground her down on the hard thrust of his erection below the denim.

And the most ridiculous thrill ran through Tansy that it was she who had aroused him, not beautiful Althea in her daring golden dress in all her extrovert attention-seeking glory. She blushed for her own petty and pathetic sense of achievement but there it was, an inescapable fact that she was as competitive when it came to Jude as any other woman. It was *her* he wanted, not his childhood sweetheart, his once-adored first love.

Bending her back over his arm to support her, he closed his lips round a swollen rosy nipple and suckled strongly. Her breathing grew choppy in her throat as he attended to the other straining peak, that heat at the heart of her spreading into a torturous ache as he ground her down on him. Long fingers laced into the fall of her hair.

'I love the different colours in your hair and I love it when you wear it loose,' Jude confided, watching the dying sun glimmer across the lighter strands where the tips touched the floor as he bent her back. 'You're also remarkably flexible—'

'Gymnastics.' Tansy laughed. 'It was much more fun than ballet classes.'

And she thought abstractedly that that had to be the true definition of a womaniser, a man capable of making her laugh in a sexual situation where she was less than confident of her body or of what happened next. His mouth brushed against hers again while his fingertips glanced expertly over the absurdly responsive tips of her breasts, tugging, gently twisting and rolling, making her squirm and moan while arrows of craving stabbed deep in her pelvis, starting up a tingling, throbbing burn between her thighs.

Without warning, Jude stood up, carrying her with him, her legs anchored round his waist. 'Let's get more comfortable,' he urged, tumbling her down on the bed, her hair fanning out wildly around her head, her green eyes huge at that sudden change of pace. 'Relax,' he urged. 'We take this as far as you want and no further.'

Tansy went pink and winced. 'Am I that easily read?'

'Pretty much, *koukla mou*.' His slanting grin of affirmation was pure charismatic gold as he stood beside the bed, hauling his shirt off over his head to reveal the defined sheet of lean muscle that corrugated his broad chest. He cast it off to embark more languidly on his jeans.

As the jeans began to fall and she realised that he was wearing nothing beneath, she stilled. A dark happy trail arrowed down to a very substantial erection. He was long and wide and she wished she had the nerve to tell him that, with every skin cell in her body jangling with a terrifying overload of sexual response, he could go as far as he liked because she was done with waiting to find out what all the fuss was about.

He came down on the bed beside her, gloriously, unashamedly masculine, and she shimmied over to him and kissed him with lingering pleasure. He smelled so good she wanted to bury her nose in him, and he tasted even better. Her hand speared into his black curls to hold him fast. A long finger scored across the taut triangle of cloth stretched between her legs and she almost spontaneously combusted from the jolt of excitement that shot through her.

Jude rolled her over and flat against the pillows, dark golden, glittering eyes hot as a predator's as he lay over her, supporting his weight on his arms. 'If we continue, do you mind if I don't use protection? Or is it too soon for you to want to try conceiving?'

Her brain was in flux and she had to struggle to grasp what he was asking, blinking up at him without immediate comprehension.

'You look like a baby bird when you look up at me like that,' Jude husked.

The concept of immediately trying for the pregnancy she had agreed to stunned her, but that there might be a fast result struck her as so off-the-charts unlikely, she couldn't even picture it. From what she had read and heard, however, it could take months to conceive, which meant that waiting too long to try could be unwise. 'It's all right with me,' she muttered.

He tugged off the thong, cast it aside, smoothed a carnal fingertip gently over the tiny bundle of nerves below her mound. The hunger awakened with extreme force and flooded her like an addictive drug, tiny nerve endings firing up for the first time, her whole body tensing and trembling as he explored her maddeningly sensitive flesh. She pressed her hot face into a satin-smooth brown shoulder, startled by the sheer pleasure thrumming through her. And then the tightening at the heart of her gave way and the world went white as she climaxed in his arms, gasping and shuddering in the aftermath.

'No matter what I do, this is probably going to hurt,' Jude murmured intently.

'I *know* that… I'm not that naive!' Tansy protested breathlessly.

'And you're very, very sexy,' Jude growled. 'Because I did intend to keep my hands off you for at least a few weeks!'

'Well, the best-laid plans…' Tansy chided with a face-splitting grin of pride, relieved that she wasn't the only one tempted in their relationship, the only one surrendering to that hunger she had never really felt until that moment.

Jude laughed, brilliant, dark, golden, heavily lashed eyes spectacular in his lean, sundarkened face. He wondered how long it had been since he had last relaxed to that extent with a woman in bed. He couldn't remember because all his more recent dealings with women had been of the most basic variety, consisting of nothing more than casual encounters.

He kissed her again with more passion and less restraint as he shifted against her, allowing her to feel the hard thrust of him against her tender core. Her heart hammered as he crushed her lips under his and she strained against him, seeking that pressure, that friction, every fibre of her demanding more sensation.

Jude pushed into her narrow channel very slowly, lifting her slight body up to him. His stunning eyes stayed welded to hers even as a low groan of sensual pleasure escaped him. '*Thee mou*...you're so tight, *moraki mou*.'

Melting within at the erotic enjoyment he couldn't hide, Tansy tipped up more to him and he slid in deeper and faster than he might have intended and she jerked as a sharp sting of pain shot through her lower body. Betrayed into a muffled moan, Tansy briefly froze. 'It's all right. Don't stop now,' she mumbled, red-faced.

Jude shifted his lithe hips and sent sweet, seductive sensations shimmying through her pelvis to replace the discomfort. Her heart thumped faster, her body quivering from that shock invasion that came with a stark jolt of pleasure and left her wanting more.

'Still hurting?' Jude pressed.

'Not any more,' she proclaimed breathlessly, rocking up into him in helpless invitation.

His fluid movements controlled her with mounting pleasure, tiny little tremors coursing through her as her tension and the ache of need built ever higher. The pace increased and her heart raced, her nails digging into the smooth skin of his back as the excitement took over, urging her hips up to his, her body jolting in satisfaction from his every powerful thrust. And then the tension splintered, and fireworks burst inside her and she was overwhelmed by the blissful convulsions of pleasure that flooded her.

Jude released her from his weight and lay back.

Tansy breathed in deep and slow, all the tension that had wound her up tight for days drained away. For the first time she felt truly close to Jude and even more regretful of the fact that she had concealed her sister's existence, starting off their marriage on a wrong note. In an effort to diminish that sin, she murmured, 'You know…er… I would have told you about Posy upfront if Calvin hadn't warned me not to.'

'At what stage did he decide to dump his daughter as well as his stepdaughter on me?' Jude enquired smooth as glass.

Tansy stiffened and compressed her lips, taken aback by his tone. She turned her head to study his taut, perfect profile. 'Nobody has been dumped on you! You needed a wife. Posy needed me. It's kind of ironic too that you're lukewarm about her, because she's truly the *only* reason I'm here with you now.'

Ebony brows drawing together, Jude locked narrowed dark golden eyes to her. 'How so?'

Tansy sighed, deciding to tell him the truth because she saw no point in concealing it any longer, and if she could improve his view of her, it could surely only make their relationship run a little more smoothly. 'It was never your money I was after. I'm not a gold-digger,' she murmured tightly. 'It was Calvin's idea. I had to agree to marry you and give my stepfather that initial financial settlement for marrying you before *he* would agree to sign over my sister into my care...'

Jude absorbed that bombshell in total silence because it plunged him deep into shock and into thoughts he did not want to have. 'Are you seriously telling me that you're planning to give *him* that money?' he demanded rawly, his lean, dark features taut with anger and incredulity. 'And that that little baby was the price of your compliance?'

Unable to grasp why that seemed to annoy him when she had naively believed that information would improve his opinion of her, Tansy sat up, hugging the sheet to her. 'Yes, and it's already done. I wouldn't have married you for any other reason... I mean, *why* else would I agree to marry a stranger? Particularly one who wanted sex included in the deal?' she countered ruefully. 'Calvin had no idea at all about that aspect. He believed you only wanted a paper marriage. But let's face it, he didn't care about the details. All he saw was an opportunity to profit.'

Jude sprang off the bed, dark colour overlaying his sharp cheekbones, rage and consternation leaping through him. 'You had sex with me because of that baby?' He stared down at her in irate disbelief.

Tansy went even more red in the face, annoyed that he didn't appear to be listening to anything she said or reacting as she had expected. 'No, I wouldn't put it that way. I wouldn't say that,' she mumbled uneasily, shying away from that too personal and private subject. 'I mean, how is that worse anyway than me being a gold-digger willing to do anything for money?'

Contrary to that protest, outrage was filling Jude to overflowing. He could see, however, that her green eyes were clear and steady on his. She didn't get it, she really *didn't* get how offensive what she had just told him was. 'You let that creepy bastard pimp you out to me like a hooker!' he accused rawly.

'How dare you?' Tansy snapped back at him in disbelief. 'How *dare* you say that to me?'

'You think I feel any warmer towards you

knowing that you only let me bed you because a child's welfare was at stake?' Jude roared. 'It didn't occur to you that that is more than a little sleazy?'

Tansy stared back at him in a fury, green eyes bright as gemstones while she struggled to conceal her hurt from him. 'Well, maybe it didn't occur to me that someone like you would be that sensitive, since you believe that you can buy *anything* you want…and you proved it with me,' she completed less boldly, still shamed by that awareness. 'But I'm not one bit sorry either!'

'I can see that,' Jude seethed, thrown off balance by her unapologetic defiance.

'Good. Then we understand each other perfectly,' Tansy told him, ripping at the sheet to wind it clumsily round herself and slide off the bed to head for the door she reckoned led to a bathroom. 'I didn't care what it cost me to get Posy out of that house and away from Calvin and his girlfriend. And unless you plan on going back on your word like *he* did, we'll adopt her now and she'll be safe, and he'll never be able to use her the way he's used me!'

And with that ringing assurance and tears

blinding her, Tansy plunged through the door only to find herself in a large dark cupboard, fitted out as a closet.

'Bathroom's next door,' Jude informed her gently as he lounged back against the tumbled bed, clad only in his unbuttoned, ripped jeans, the dark dangerous rage still smouldering in him but restrained by the innate caution of a man who had seen, growing up, what a man's unfettered ire could do to a woman. 'Couldn't get permission to knock a door through in a protected building.'

Feeling even more foolish, Tansy stalked down the corridor, trailing the sheet and stifling a sob. Her first sexual experience had come complete with a distressing aftermath. There had been no reassuring physical closeness, no show of affection. That was stuff a woman could only hope to receive from a guy who cared about her. Jude had treated her like a one-night stand because he didn't see her as being any different, indeed might even see her as being less after what she had revealed about Calvin and Posy. Her heart squeezed inside her as she worried about what the future might hold with Jude when he was that furious with her…

CHAPTER SEVEN

JUDE BREATHED IN slow and deep to calm himself.

Calvin Hetherington had to be dealt with first. No way should he profit from the morally unforgivable arrangement he had set up! That poor baby, Jude reflected with deep repugnance that a father could place such little value on his own flesh and blood. As for Tansy, she suffered from tunnel vision where her sister was concerned. She had not even paused to consider that Jude might not be as corrupt as her stepfather, had not even contemplated telling Jude the truth until the die had been cast. And now he had to sort the mess out and he needed the details to accomplish that feat. Digging out his phone, he contacted his top-notch Greek lawyer, Dmitri, and made him aware of the situation, gritting his teeth when the older man came close to questioning his judgement in entering such a marriage without having taken due consideration and care.

Jude already knew that he had been reckless. It was an Alexandris trait, but it was the first time ever that *he* had committed that sin. Maddeningly, he had only become reckless after he had first laid eyes on Tansy and she'd turned him down, he acknowledged grimly. He had wanted her the instant he'd seen her, the light glimmering over her long streaky hair, those luminous green eyes wary and anxious, the pulse beating out her nerves at the base of her elegant white throat. And Tansy had spoken the truth when she had accused him of being accustomed to buying anything he wanted, and he had bought himself a wife with no more forethought than a man buying a product off a shelf. That was a sobering truth. What right did he have now to complain about the complications Tansy had brought with her? Dmitri had warned him that it was even possible that, after he contacted the British legal team to check the facts, he would have to start paperwork to safeguard the baby by applying to have Posy made a ward of the court.

While Jude ruminated about what complications might lie ahead and sank entirely naturally into problem-solving mode, Tansy was being a lot less productive. In the spacious shower she let the pent-up tears stream down her face under the cover of the water. Posy was safe now, wasn't she? That was the all-important bottom line, wasn't it? Only she hadn't been quite truthful with Jude when she had acted as though her sister had been her only motivation. She hadn't intended to play the martyr, but she had been even less keen to admit that she found him incredibly attractive and had been intrigued and fascinated by him from the outset. Ought she to admit that? Why should she expose herself to that extent?

A knock sounded on the bathroom door while she was splashing cold water on her face in an effort to chase the puffiness of tears from her eyes. 'Yes?' she called loudly.

'Dinner in ten minutes,' Jude told her.

Tansy swallowed hard and waited a few moments before dashing back to the bedroom in a towel. A single case sat there, and she dug into it, rustling through the neatly packed garments to extract a long cotton skirt and a light strappy top. She dressed in haste, combing out her wet hair, scrutinising her wan face with critical eyes, rubbing her cheeks for some colour and then scolding herself for even caring about her appearance around Jude. After all, he was on another level of gorgeous and always would be and she was never going to catch up. Had Jude not needed a wife he could sign up on a temporary basis, he would never have considered someone as ordinary as she was for the role.

As she reached the foot of the stairs, a small, older Greek woman stepped into view and greeted her and moved forward to open a door and show her the way. Smiling politely, striving to conceal her nervous tension, Tansy stepped out onto a terrace and looked in wonder at all the fairy lights strung up above the table and the tea lights burning everywhere, illuminating the walled courtyard and the box-edged beds of herbs planted within its boundaries that sweetly scented the air. Jude leapt up from his seat, his visible discomfiture at the celebratory bridal setting almost making Tansy laugh.

'Oh, how pretty the table looks!' she exclaimed for her companion's benefit, because someone had gone to a lot of trouble stringing up those lights and setting out all those little candles.

Jude spoke in rapid Greek to her companion and the woman beamed happily at Tansy. As she vanished back indoors, Jude lounged back against the low wall edging the terrace, his long powerful legs splayed in tailored chinos. Tansy blinked, freshly assaulted by his vibrant sexuality, mortifying heat blossoming low in her body at the recollection of just how intimate their connection had been only an hour earlier.

'We have to discuss your arrangement with your stepfather,' Jude informed her, sending her thoughts crashing back to practical issues again. 'Did he somehow grant you legal custody of Posy?'

Tansy's face dropped in dismay at that direct and precise question and she shook her head. 'He assured me beforehand that he would, but that turned out to be a lie and we got married so fast I didn't pick up on it until it was too late. He told me that the only way I could have legal custody of my sister was by adopting her and, of course, that would mean that you had to be part of the application as well.'

Jude looked unsurprised by her explanation. 'His deception was calculated. He won't want to surrender custody of his daughter while he thinks he could still use her as a blackmail tool.'

Her smooth brow indented. 'How?'

Jude sprang upright and reached for the bottle of champagne awaiting their attention, unsealing it with a pop and filling the glasses. 'Hetherington could demand that you return his daughter to him...or that you compensate him accordingly. As my wife, you have access to a great deal of money.'

'I wouldn't let him *do* that!' Tansy protested heatedly.

'You've already demonstrated that there isn't much you wouldn't sacrifice in order to keep your sister with you,' Jude reminded her sardonically. 'Including your virginity.'

In the act of tossing back the bubbling champagne, Tansy almost choked on it while the heat of embarrassment enveloped her entire body. 'I've already told you...it wasn't like that. But I assure you that I have no plans to hand over any more of your money to Calvin. That would be like *stealing* from you.'

'Then it will be good news for you to hear that Calvin has yet to receive a penny of what you describe as *my* money,' Jude retorted crisply. 'But that sum was yours to do with as you wish. It became yours the day you married me.'

'As I told you, I've already transferred that money to Calvin,' Tansy muttered uncomfortably.

'You tried to but, ultimately, the transaction was blocked.'

'*Blocked?*' she echoed in dismay.

'Our bank accounts are heavily protected from fraud. Such a large transfer as emptying your new bank account was flagged and would have been run by me before it was allowed to proceed. Now it's permanently blocked. Hetherington is not going to get that money.'

'But then I bet he'll demand Posy back!' Tansy gasped. 'I *agreed* to give him that money.'

'Just as he agreed to give you legal custody of your sister, which he didn't,' Jude reminded her drily. 'He's *not* getting that money, Tansy.

Fathers aren't allowed to sell their children in today's world. Furthermore, any money changing hands between you and your stepfather would invalidate any adoption proceedings in the future as it would be illegal. No, we will deal with your stepfather together and only through the proper legal channels.'

'But that'll put Posy staying with us at risk and I couldn't *b-bear* to lose her!' Tansy framed with a stifled sob of sudden fear half under her breath.

'We won't lose her,' Jude swore. 'I won't allow that to happen. That's the least of what I owe you.'

'You don't owe me anything, Jude. I brought Posy into this marriage without your knowledge. You're not responsible for what happens to her—'

'You're my wife. She's your blood relative. She's entitled to my protection. I also have an engrained loathing for greedy, dishonest operators like your stepfather and no child deserves a parent that heartless.' Jude yanked out a chair and gently nudged her towards it. 'Sit down. Our housekeeper, Olympia, is about to serve our meal, *moli mou.*'

'I'm not sure I could eat.' A shaky smile

formed on Tansy's lips. 'You probably don't understand but I love Posy as much as though she was born to me. I was the first person to hold her after her birth and she's been mine to care for ever since.'

'What sort of stepfather was Calvin before your mother died?' Jude asked her, surprising her with that question.

Tansy compressed her lips. 'Absent, uninterested. Mum and him just led their lives and I got on with mine at school and when they went on holiday I moved in with my aunt Violet.'

'And your mother. What was she like?'

Her sense of wonder lingered, along with a growing pleasure that he was keen to know such facts about her. She wasn't used to talking about herself but there was a heady feeling of satisfaction inside her at being the sole focus of his interest.

'She was wrapped up in Calvin and very conscious that she was ten years older than he was,' Tansy confided wryly. 'That's why she was overjoyed when she fell pregnant. Neither of them had expected that but I could see he didn't share her enthusiasm. He never wanted a child. I think he married Mum because she struck him as a good financial bet. She owned her own home and business. But if you can believe what he told me, they were living well above their means and he's currently facing bankruptcy.'

'What did you inherit?'

'Nothing. Mum left everything to Calvin. If he hadn't needed someone to look after Posy, he would never have allowed me to stay on in the house for so long,' she pointed out ruefully. 'I mean, it's not like he or I were ever close or that there was any family tie.'

'And your own father?' Jude prompted.

Tansy ate the last delicious bite of the starter and set down her cutlery, surprised by how hungry she had been. She lifted her champagne glass. 'He was an accountant and he died in a car accident when I was a baby. He was a lot older than Mum. I have no memory of him at all, but he left Mum quite well off. She opened up a beauty salon and lived well on the income…well, at least until she and Calvin got together.'

'A beauty salon?' Jude was disconcerted because there was nothing remotely artificial about Tansy and, to his way of thinking, artifice flourished in beauty salons.

'And it made no impression on me... I *know*.' Tansy laughed, her small straight nose wrinkling. 'But if you'd met my mother you'd soon have guessed what the family business was. She had every beauty enhancement on the market and wouldn't have opened the front door without her false eyelashes on. I was a *huge* disappointment! She wanted a daughter who was just like her and, although I did all the training courses to please her and worked at the salon whenever I was needed, it never interested me the way it did her.'

The main course arrived, and Tansy realised she had been chattering nonstop about herself and she flushed and fell silent.

'I was saving the main question until last,' Jude murmured softly as he watched her, entranced by her pale porcelain skin and delicate features, the strap of the top she wore sliding off one slender shoulder. 'Why was such a beautiful girl still sexually innocent?'

Tansy dragged in a long, quivering breath, unable to accept that he saw her as beautiful, suddenly plunged into horrible awkwardness by such a query. 'I'm not going to talk about that on the grounds that it makes me feel like a fool and as days go, this has already been a very long and trying one.'

As her voice fell away Jude simply spread long fingers in an accepting gesture, although he knew that he would be revisiting that topic. 'You'll be reunited with your sister tomorrow. My yacht is travelling here overnight.'

'Your…yacht?' Tansy repeated.

'*The Alexandris*—my twenty-fifth birthday present from Isidore,' Jude told her flatly.

'Pretty over the top as gifts go, but then, as you said, he is that way inclined. But even so, he's enormously attached to you. I could see that.'

Jude glanced across the table with startled dark golden eyes. 'You *could*?'

Tansy marvelled at his inky black lashes and the length of them and stiffened at that abstracted thought, shifting in her seat and feeling the soreness at her still-tender core, the legacy of that new experience he had mentioned. Her face burned as she fought to concentrate on the conversation. 'Yes, it's obvious. He's proud of you. It shines out of him every time he looks at you,' she muttered ruefully.

Jude had never thought of Isidore, his grandfather, as being personally fond of him. For most of his life, albeit secretly, he had viewed his family history from his mother's side of the fence and had seen both his father and his grandfather as ruthless, often cruel predators with few saving graces, who saw in him only that all-important necessity: the heir to the Alexandris wealth to be groomed to follow in their footsteps. Had he been blind or was Tansy naive and mistaken?

He shook off that wandering thought, acknowledging the armour he had put on from childhood once he'd understood that his father, Dion, didn't expect him to get emotional about anything because an Alexandris male only expressed violent anger. Dion had been unable to control that anger as Isidore did, and Jude could remember his father raging at staff, at office workers, at his cowering mother, in truth at anyone who ignited his hair-trigger temper. Dion Alexandris had had all the self-control of a spoilt and indulged toddler and, having witnessed that, Jude had learned young to control his anger. In a real rage, Jude turned to ice.

As they ate the main course, Jude talked about the yacht and Tansy giggled at some of the revealing extras that his grandfather had thought to include, like a stripper pole, a giant hot tub and mirrored ceilings. 'Not really my style,' Jude insisted. 'But Isidore and my father were the ultimate playboys back in the days of their youth.'

Unimpressed by the claim, Tansy rolled her bright eyes. 'I'm pretty sure you're not that innocent.'

'I'm not, but I was only a man-whore for a couple of years after Althea when I was wrapped up in being bitter as hell,' Jude admitted. 'I'm an adult. I got over it eventually.'

'But by the sounds of it, your father never did,' Tansy slotted in before she could think better about getting that personal.

'That's how he was raised. Any woman he wanted he should have, regardless of whether or not he was married or with anyone else. He bedded my mother's sister, her maid, my nanny,' Jude enumerated drily.

Tansy was truly shocked but fought to hide the fact. 'I don't think much of a sister that would do that.'

'You'd be surprised how easily tempted people can be to do unforgivable things,' Jude murmured very seriously. 'I should've been less honest…you're shocked.'

'I thought Calvin was bad when he brought a woman home for the night less than a month after my mother passed,' Tansy muttered uncomfortably. 'I just ignored it, acted like it wasn't happening because I didn't have any alternative.'

'Hetherington didn't ever come on to you?' Jude prompted tautly.

'Oh, my goodness, no!' Tansy laughed outright at the idea. 'That's one sin he didn't commit. I'm not his type, though. His type is big blond mane of hair, large boobs, very decorative. Didn't you see his girlfriend outside the register office? Susie is like a much younger version of my mother.'

Olympia brought coffee. Jude stepped away from the table and sank back down with careless grace on the wall to survey Tansy with an intensity that made her uneasy. He had beautiful eyes, but they could also be very piercing and distinctly intimidating.

'What?' she said defensively, as though he had spoken.

'Now we have to talk about the elephant in the room…the topic you don't want to touch,'

Jude extended softly. 'I want to know *why* you had sex with me this evening. And I need an *honest* answer. I think I deserve that from you.'

Caught unprepared by that demand, Tansy was aghast at his candour; her lips rounded and her eyes were huge and green with stricken dismay. 'I… I—'

'You need to think about it?' Jude elevated a sardonic ebony brow. 'Really? Nobody should need to think *that* hard about telling the truth.'

And that genuinely put Tansy in the hot seat and she sat as stiff and expressionless as a statue in her chair. 'I can't even understand why you would be asking me that question,' she argued.

'From what I understand, Hetherington virtually blackmailed you into agreeing to marry me. You wanted to protect your sister and that's why you agreed…correct?'

Tansy nodded as jerkily as a marionette hanging taut on uneven strings.

'How do you think *I* feel knowing that you were pressured into sharing my bed?'

'But you didn't pressure me…*not at all*!' Tansy stressed in fierce disagreement.

'That doesn't add up. Before we married you asked me to give you time to get to know me,' Jude reminded her, causing hot colour to sweep into her cheeks. 'Then we marry, you produce Posy like a rabbit out of a hat and then all of a sudden you decide you don't need getting-to-know-me time and we have sex. Was that because you felt you had to please or soothe me in some way to persuade me to accept your sister?' Jude demanded with all the cool, critical fire of a hanging judge.

'No!' Tansy slashed back at him in a temper at being mortified to such an extent. 'I had sex with you because, *stupidly*, after you confided in me about Althea, I felt closer to you because someone I cared about was once unfaithful to me as well. Why the hell should you even need an explanation for why I chose to be with you?'

'Because I will not accept an unwilling partner.'

'I wasn't unwilling, you stupid, *stupid* man!' Tansy launched back at him in a towering rage such as she had never, ever felt before. 'I just like you...*why else* would I have broken my own rule?'

Jude froze as though she had struck him

and he was, she reckoned, lucky that in her anger she hadn't lashed out physically, because she felt absolutely humiliated at being forced to go into the reasons why she had succumbed to his irrefutable attraction. In all her life she had never felt sexual chemistry as powerful as what she felt around him, had never even dreamt that a guy could affect her with one look or one touch the way Jude did. And it truly was scarcely a mystery that, married off at speed to an absolutely beautiful, sexy man, she had succumbed to that irresistible attraction. Only a complete idiot would have required such a fact spelt out to him!

'I'm not stupid.' Jude caught her hands in his as she attempted to move past him and walk indoors. 'I simply had to know whether or not you were with me because you wanted to be and not because you felt you *had* to be.'

Face burning, Tansy flung back her head and slung him an angry, mutinous glance. 'Well, *now* you know! I hope it was a moment worth embarrassing me for to this extent!'

Scorching golden eyes smouldered down at her. 'I'm sorry—'

'No, you're not!' Tansy argued helplessly because she could see a positively platinum glow of satisfaction shining from him. 'You heard exactly what you wanted to hear, only you can't have *needed* to hear it.'

'It never mattered so much before,' Jude framed, gripping her small hands tight when she tried to break free of him.

'In a few seconds I am going to kick you very hard,' Tansy warned him between clenched teeth.

In a sleight of hand and at a speed that took her utterly by surprise, Jude released her hands and bent down to scoop her up into his arms instead. A disconcerted squeak escaped Tansy before his warm, sensual lips engulfed hers and he tasted so good her head spun, her toes curled. The pulse of hunger renewed, disconcerting her because she had thought that crazy, clawing need was sated. After all, her body still ached, and yet when Jude tumbled her down on the wide bed and kissed her breathless, she wanted him again with a wildness that shocked her. The heat in her pelvis induced a craving that she couldn't fight.

Her fingers raked through his hair, her body lifting in delight to the weight and hardness of his, hands sliding down over his back, that insane excitement building and building to an incredible height and making her feel shameless and greedy.

'I can't get enough of you!' Jude growled, burying his mouth in the soft, sensitive skin between her nape and her shoulder, letting her feel his teeth and sending shock waves of arousal coursing through her.

'Is it always like this?' she mumbled dizzily, angling back her head to allow him easier access to the tender slopes of her unbound breasts.

'Are you kidding?' Jude laughed, unholy amusement illuminating the dark golden eyes locked to her face, colour lying along his high cheekbones. 'If it was always like this for me, I'd be a sex fiend!'

CHAPTER EIGHT

POSY'S CHUCKLES SHOOK her squirming little body as she rolled away from being tickled and crawled under the desk, peering up at Jude with bright blue eyes brimming with merriment as he flung himself back into his office chair with a grin of amusement at his own behaviour.

Never having had anything to do with children before, Jude had not even considered that he could be fascinated by a baby, but he had discovered that the very simplicity and lack of guile in so young a child appealed to him. Posy liked or disliked stuff or people. There were no shades of grey with her, nothing fake. She didn't care who he was or what he could give her as long as he played with her and made her feel safe and appreciated.

He had been married to Tansy for six weeks and, very much to his surprise and in defiance of his ingrained cynicism, Jude was extremely satisfied with the wife he had picked and the life they were sharing. Tansy was a breath of fresh air in his world. Watching her with Posy, he was impressed by her warmth and affection for the child and the sacrifices she had been willing to make to keep Posy in her care. She didn't have a gold-digging gene in her entire body. When he had presented her with a phone she had been shocked to realise that the blue and white diamonds on the case were real and had tried to return it to him. She had even lectured him about how appalling it was to *waste* that amount of money on a phone, because she had yet to grasp that, on his terms, what he had spent was *not* a huge amount of money.

On a practical basis, Tansy was perfect. As for the 'having a child' part of his marriage, Jude had, for the present, pretty much buried that ambition at the back of his mind. Of course, he reflected, it *would* be helpful to his future plans if a conception took place, but it could also change things in his relationship with Tansy and, right at that moment, Jude wanted nothing to change because he liked it just as it was. Indeed, he liked it a whole hell of a lot. Their sex life was off-the-charts fantastic. He couldn't keep his hands off Tansy and she was pretty much the same with him. He had never enjoyed that level of sexual chemistry with a woman before and that told him that it had to be incredibly hard to find that enhanced buzz and thrill, because he was no innocent. His liberal upbringing and his opportunities had made his sexual experience a fact of life.

'Are you tormenting my sister again?' Tansy teased as she walked into his office and discovered that there wasn't a lot of work getting done just at that moment. A colourful cascade of toddler toys lay scattered across the rug. Safe playing spaces suitable for a baby had appeared all over the magnificent yacht after Posy had slid and banged her head on a hard wooden floor. *The Alexandris* had not been designed with a baby in mind and Jude had had to ensure that, where possible, the vessel was child-friendly for her sister's benefit.

'She's much more fun than a coffee break,' Jude informed her with gravity, his lean, strong face full of contrasting amusement. From his flaring black brows, bronzed skin, lion-gold eyes and taut jaw line, he remained as spectacular as a living, breathing vision to Tansy's admiring gaze.

Turning pink, Tansy reflected on how very far their relationship had progressed over the past six weeks. All three of them had travelled an impossible distance from that difficult start, not least her baby sister, currently engaged in trying to climb onto Jude's chair with him to regain his attention. Posy adored Jude. The little girl squirmed and slid back down again and started to cry and Jude reached down a long arm and automatically hauled the baby up. Posy clambered across his lap with a beaming smile, sat down, rested her curly head calmly back against his chest and stuck her thumb in her rosebud mouth, her satisfaction unconcealed.

'Although she's not quite as much fun as you are, *moli mou*,' Jude intoned thickly, lushly lashed dark golden eyes narrowing to wander over her slight body. His intense gaze lingered on the soft pink fullness of her mouth, the sun-streaked fall of her hair and the pouting profile of her breasts in a halter-neck top before literally devouring the long, smooth, golden length of her legs in casual denim shorts.

And below that scorching appraisal, which was now so awesomely familiar to her, Tansy's whole body lit up like a torch with heat and awareness. Her nipples tightened, something clenched low in her pelvis and her insides turned liquid and melting.

A knock sounded on the door and Posy's nanny appeared. Jude sprang upright and passed over the sleepy child, crossing the floor as the door closed again to tug Tansy up against his tall, powerful frame. One hand wound into the thick, silky length of her hair to tip her head back and the other flirted with the fashionably frayed edges of her shorts so that she quivered against him, as on edge as a cat on hot coals.

He crushed her mouth under his, his tongue delving deep, and a low whimper of helpless response escaped low in her throat. 'We only got out of bed a few hours ago,' Jude grated above her head, bumping his brow against hers in apology while she struggled to breathe again. 'This is crazy.'

'Yes, it is,' Tansy muttered, trying to call

a halt on her own runaway hormones. 'We shouldn't give in to it.'

Jude ground the thrust of his arousal into her stomach. 'To hell with self-denial,' he groaned raggedly.

'You're not into that,' she conceded shakily.

He tipped up her chin to gaze down at her. 'Are you too sore? Oh, don't go all shy about it. I *know* I'm demanding.'

'You're not too demanding,' Tansy framed, biting at her full lower lip, her face rosy. 'I would tell you if—'

'The same way you would tell me why you were still a virgin when I married you?' Jude scorned, unimpressed. 'If you're embarrassed, you won't tell me anything.'

'Right… OK. I'll tell you why I was inexperienced…*later*,' she promised reluctantly.

'It's a deal.' Jude treated her to one of his wide, charismatic smiles that dazzled her. 'It annoys me when you won't tell me things.'

'I know, but I'm getting better,' she pointed out. 'I just never had anyone to confide in before.'

And the very thought of what she had just admitted hit her like a resounding crash of doom. What did it say about her that she was confiding in a fake husband as if he were the real thing? A loving, affectionate guy, who was intending to stay with her? That awful truth was so clear to her but, even so, somehow all her boundaries with Jude had blurred and every time she tried to take a sensible step back from him he inexplicably contrived to yank her closer.

That they had spent the past six weeks behaving like a *real* couple on a honeymoon certainly didn't help her to retain rational barriers. Initially she had been overwhelmed by the giant yacht and the sheer luxury of its appointments, but somewhere along the line, she conceded guiltily, she had become accustomed to living with meals served whenever hunger struck, a maid, a team of nannies and an onboard beauty salon where she could have her hair done any time she liked. And with all the practicalities of life taken care of for her, so much time had been freed up, time she had spent with Posy and Jude while *The Alexandris* sailed round the Greek islands, stopping off wherever took their fancy.

As he yanked the door open again, Jude closed a hand over hers and they headed down the passageway and up the stairs to their gorgeous cabin. For a split second Tansy tried to break free of that sensual haze that entrapped her, but, one step into complete privacy, Jude scooped her off her feet and tumbled her down on the bed and the allure of the sheer excitement he sent cascading through her overwhelmed her again. Heart hammering inside her chest, she exchanged kiss for kiss as they rolled across the bed, engaged in a frantic effort to rid themselves of their clothing and connect at the fastest rate possible.

There was nothing cool about that urge, nothing controlled or disciplined. In fact, the insanity that often seemed to grip her in Jude's radius bewildered Tansy as much as it dominated her, because she had no previous experience of the woman she became with Jude. She ripped at his shirt, pressed her lips hungrily to a satin-smooth brown shoulder and trembled at the aphrodisiac of his scent. She couldn't get enough of him, couldn't deny the needs of her own body. The instant he touched her she went up in flames. He was *her* source of irresistible temptation and she wanted to savour every moment with him just as feverishly as she told herself that she needed to learn to control her susceptibility.

Skilled fingers traced the sensitive skin at her core and she jerked, frantically opening her mouth to the delve of his tongue. All of her was on fire, the tips of her breasts straining and stiff, the heart of her damp and pulsing. He flipped her over as easily as though she were a doll and ground into her hard and fast and the pleasure was almost more than she could bear. She arched her back and moaned, the delight of pure unvarnished sensation screaming through every fibre of her being. Her climax still quivering through her limp body, Tansy finally flopped back against the sheets, absolutely wiped out by the experience.

With a glimmering smile, Jude reached for her and drew her under a strong arm, disconcerting her so much for a moment that she froze.

'What's up?' Jude prompted.

'Nothing, absolutely nothing,' she hastened to tell him, as though that small affectionate gesture were an everyday occurrence.

It wasn't. Jude didn't cuddle or snuggle or hug after sex. He was very much an island, a loner in intimacy. From the sidelines she had watched him slowly, almost clumsily learning to respond to Posy's unrestrained baby affection. She had seen him freeze in shock the first time her sister dabbed playful baby kisses all over his face in the same game she often played with Tansy. But Posy had forged her own path with Jude and he was returning her hugs without restraint now, and it seemed as though that had changed something in him, Tansy acknowledged with quiet pleasure, ridiculously pleased by that arm anchoring her to him in the aftermath. Why? It gave her a sense of achievement and the conviction that she was humanising Jude, who could often seem remote from the concerns that troubled others.

'So,' Jude murmured softly. 'You agreed to tell me why...'

'Is that why you're hugging me for the first time ever?' Tansy demanded with sudden anger. 'You want me to bare my soul, so you come over all manipulative and finally hug me?'

A frown line drawing his ebony brows together, Jude studied her in apparent wonderment. 'You will be *"baring your soul"*?' he queried.

Tansy went red. 'Well, that was a bit of an exaggeration,' she conceded, marvelling and mortified that that angry outburst had emerged from her without her volition.

'But the use of that word, "finally", suggests that I'm a major fail in the hug department?' Jude pressed. 'Well, that's not surprising. I didn't get hugged as a child very often—'

'But surely your mother—'

'No, when she visited me after losing custody of me to my father, she wasn't allowed to touch me. Isidore and my father hated her and considered her a malign influence and restricted her access to me as much as they could,' he took her aback by revealing. 'A nanny with strict instructions always acted as a chaperone.'

'But why on earth did they hate her so much?' Tansy exclaimed, wide-eyed.

'I think because she fought back and wouldn't lie down to be walked over. All their lives Isidore and my father were all-powerful in almost every sphere and virtually everyone set out to please them. To be fair to them, though, Clio can be very difficult to deal with. In the end they dealt with her by almost destroying her,' he breathed tautly. 'But we're not going to get distracted by my background just when you were about to spill the beans about why you were still a virgin when we met.'

Tansy gritted her teeth at the reminder and lay as still as a statue beside him. Her mind was still clinging to what he had told her about his background though. Growing up in such a difficult family situation had damaged Jude too. She was trying to imagine his childhood without hugs and winced in sympathy. The adults around him had been at daggers drawn and he had suffered accordingly. Distrust and intolerance had deprived Jude of the loving care he should have enjoyed.

Certainly, Tansy had had a better experience as a young child, but her face shadowed when she recalled her teenaged years when her peers had been dating and getting sexual experience. By that stage, the lack of understanding and shared interests between Tansy and her mother had become more obvious. She admitted to Jude that she had never had time at that age to get out and about. Either she had been swotting for exams, off on a beauty training course or working in her mother's salon.

'There wasn't room for anything else in my life.' She sighed. 'And in any case, nobody was interested in me that way.'

'I don't believe that.'

Tansy rolled her eyes, unimpressed, thinking back to her almost prepubescent lack of curves in her teens. 'When I started university I was sharing a flat with five girls. For the first time I was having a social life. The others were much more comfortable with boys than I was, and they all had active sex lives. I didn't realise it at the time but afterwards, after what happened, I think a few of those girls disliked me just for being different. Early on I admitted I was a virgin but that I was hoping to meet someone special. I was teased a lot, but I didn't let it bother me.'

'Why should you have?' Jude breathed above her head.

'One of my flatmates became my best friend, a girl called Emma. I fell madly in love with Ben, who was on Emma's course, and we started dating. I was quite frank with him about not being willing to jump into bed with him straight away. I wanted to see if we could go anywhere first,' Tansy admitted ruefully. 'I suppose that was pretty naive…me expecting him to wait.'

'No. It was his choice, whether he did or not,' Jude chipped in, being more supportive than she had expected.

'We were dating a few months and I was so *happy*,' Tansy recited with a groan of embarrassment. 'He was my first boyfriend and we were holding hands! And then one weekend, when I was supposed to be going home, I accidentally found out the *real* truth of what was going on behind my back. Mum cancelled my visit at the last minute because she and Calvin had been invited away by friends. I returned to the flat unexpectedly and found Emma and Ben in bed together and heard them laughing about me.'

Jude turned her face towards him as she fell silent. 'What did you do?'

'I confronted them. Emma admitted they'd been together from the start and that she and her friends and his had bet Ben that he couldn't collect my V-card,' Tansy confessed stiltedly. 'They'd all set me up for a joke. I was horrified, humiliated, awfully hurt because, not only did I love Ben, I believed Emma was my best friend.'

'I bet Ben tried to get you back afterwards,' Jude surprised her by remarking.

Tansy frowned. 'He acted like a freaking stalker… I couldn't believe that after what he'd done he could even think I'd have anything more to do with him! How did you know that he did that?'

'Because I'm a man and I would assume he was simply using Emma for sex until he got you. He wouldn't have wasted all that time on you if he hadn't been keen. I would also suggest that she was in love with Ben too and jealous of his attraction to you,' Jude summed up with confidence.

'And what made you the teenage love guru?' Tansy whispered, turning over to look at him, her heart tightening. 'A very misspent youth?'

'I was with Althea. There was nothing misspent about my youth,' Jude reminded her wryly. 'That's why I went off the rails after her. I felt like an idiot for looking for *"for ever"* when everyone around me the same age was settling for a "just for now" option.'

Tansy smoothed a possessive hand down

over his well-defined abs, honed to perfection as she knew by daily early morning gym sessions, which she often shared although her passion was running. 'I think that's admirable, that you rejected the life your father and grandfather had led and set your heart on something more lasting.'

'No, it was naive, stupid,' Jude argued. 'I was too young to know what I was doing—'

'No,' Tansy continued to disagree. 'You just picked the wrong girl.'

An involuntary laugh escaped Jude. 'You make it sound so simple.'

'Sometimes it is. Someone like me would have appreciated your values,' Tansy muttered, engaged in kissing a haphazard line down over his rippling stomach, one small hand tracing a long muscular thigh.

'Yes, but we're not in this long-term, are we?' Jude muttered thickly, one hand sliding into her hair, keen to urge her in the right direction, unashamed lust gripping him with need all over again. 'So that angle doesn't come into it.'

Momentarily, Tansy froze and tried to make herself continue what she was doing, but it was impossible when she felt as though

Jude had dropped a giant rock on her from a height, squashing breath and hope from her as he forced her back into the world of reality, rather than the world of fantasy where she had been getting rather too comfortable.

'My goodness, I'm starving!' she exclaimed, sitting up suddenly, rescuing herself.

Jude frowned, not an easy man to deflect, and he caught her hand before she could move off the bed. 'What did I say?'

Her fine-featured face froze. 'You didn't say anything.'

'About us not being long-term?' Jude pressed. 'But that's a *fact*.'

'Yes, of course, it is,' Tansy agreed, still trying to work out how best to evade that awkward subject.

Jude scrutinised her with shrewd dark golden eyes. 'Don't get attached to me, *moli mou*. I'm a bad bet.'

Tansy flipped her rippling hair off the side of her face with a steady hand. 'I wouldn't get attached to you. You're not my type,' she replied flatly.

'How can you say that?' Jude demanded, thoroughly disconcerted by that reply, and spreading lean brown hands to indicate the tumbled bed she had just slid off as if it were evidence to the contrary.

Tansy steeled herself to stand where she was, naked and vulnerable and seemingly unconcerned. 'That's simple chemistry and basically meaningless,' she downplayed, reaching for a robe with studious calm.

'We'll be flying back to Athens for my birthday party tomorrow. Isidore insisted. He always insists on throwing me a party,' Jude imparted ruefully. 'One would think that a thirtieth celebration could be left for me to enjoy in my own way.'

'But listening to you, one would also think how very spoilt and entitled you are,' Tansy incised thinly. 'Nobody ever threw a party for *me* in my entire life! Your grandfather loves and cares about you. For goodness' sake, the man's on the phone to you every day, interested in every breath that you take! What does it take for you to appreciate what you have?'

Colour scored Jude's high cheekbones. He clenched his teeth together on an acerbic response. Tansy viewed his family through a different scope, possibly because she had been pretty much neglected by her own mother, he reasoned inwardly. Tansy had never been put first or spoiled or indulged by a proud or loving parent. But he *had* been, Jude registered for possibly the first time, thinking of how every household he had lived in from childhood had revolved around him and of how Isidore had scrupulously made time for him whenever his father was unavailable. It was strange how Tansy's opinions were changing his outlook on some areas of his life, he acknowledged uneasily.

Isidore had instilled his grandson with the belief that women were innately untrustworthy, probably in the hope of driving another wedge between Jude and his mother. After Althea had proved Isidore's theory, Jude had strongly resisted the concept of being influenced by any woman. As for love, he was never doing that again, that went without saying. He got by fine without love, had done so for years. But the suggestion that he might have been blind to the reality that his grandfather loved him pierced him on a deep level, cutting through the barriers that his mother had set up inside his head when he was much younger. He wasn't enjoying Tansy's insight into his family as an onlooker, but it was certainly making him think for the first time in a long time about how his dysfunctional background could have moved certain facts weirdly out of focus.

'I appreciate what I have,' Jude countered ruefully. 'Enough serious talk though…let's concentrate on what you're wearing for the party. It will be a very glitzy event.'

Tansy nodded with a jerk and vanished into the palatial en suite bathroom, her eyes burning with moisture. He had warned her not to get attached to him. He had missed the boat, Tansy reflected wretchedly. She had done what she had believed she would not do, had let feelings take hold, because it would *never* be just chemistry for her with Jude. There was just so much she liked and appreciated about him that he made her head spin.

Foremost in that line was his uncompromising honesty and his compassion for his troubled mother, whom he rarely saw. Then there was his quick and intelligent brain, because there was no denying that a clever man was the most entertaining and the best company. His kindness towards Posy, his lack of snobbishness when Tansy sometimes got things wrong because she had grown up at another social level, his generosity with other people because, for someone she had called spoilt, he was remarkably tolerant. She could have kept listing admirable attributes for longer, she conceded while she stood in the shower, letting the tears finally fall, but what was the point?

She had fallen in love with a guy who would never love her back and that broke her heart. She had nothing to hope for either, when their arrangement excluded love in favour of practicality. Jude had ringed their entire relationship with boundaries. In addition, she felt guilty about loving him, about having failed to keep emotion out of their agreement while at the same time Jude was fully meeting his end of the deal to be a father to Posy. How could she complain when she had caught feelings for him? He had specifically warned her against getting attached to him. He had, in short, given her exactly what he had promised, and it would be ridiculously naive of her to hope for anything more permanent when he had been so candid from the outset…

CHAPTER NINE

'IT'S GORGEOUS,' TANSY whispered as Jude clasped the fragile emerald and diamond necklace at her nape.

'And this set isn't an Alexandris heirloom which you can only borrow. It's yours,' Jude stressed, sending a shard of pain winging through her that he felt as though he had to make that fine distinction because she *wasn't* a genuine Alexandris wife, with him for the long haul.

A fixed smile in place, Tansy shifted her head so that the matching earrings shimmered in the light. 'It's a really beautiful gift. Thank you very much,' she murmured quietly. 'But I don't know when I would ever wear it again after we're divorced. I can't see me living the high life.'

Jude's lean, strong face clenched hard. He might have warned Tansy not to get too attached to being his wife, but he didn't like it when she referred to their eventual divorce… particularly as though it were just a heartbeat away when it *wasn't*! Strangely, that outlook of hers should have been welcome but instead it set his teeth on edge. They had been together less than a couple of months, yet, all of a sudden, Tansy seemed to be racing for the finishing line as though she couldn't wait to get away from him.

Yes, virtually overnight something had definitely *changed* in Tansy because she was on edge and curiously quiet. All day he had been struggling to get her to talk and relax the way she usually did. Her new reserve made him tense and made him question his own behaviour and it was already driving him absolutely crazy.

Tansy cast a last glance at her reflection in the cheval mirror. Jude's birthday party was a very formal event. The green ballgown with its beautiful stylish embroidery glittered with crystals in the dusk light. It hugged her slender figure like a glove, fanning out below her knees in a profusion of fabric above high-heeled sandals the exact same colour.

'You look like a Venus…it's outrageously

sexy,' Jude intoned huskily, long fingers stroking down her slender spine.

Her breath caught in her throat and she quivered, but still she stepped away, practising the self-denial he had once mocked. 'I'm not curvy enough for that comparison.'

'Curvy enough from what I can see, *moraki mou*,' Jude remarked with amusement, narrowed eyes resting pointedly on the delicate but full pout of her bosom below the fitted dress.

My goodness, had he noticed that she had got a little bigger there? Tansy frowned, suspecting that she needed new bras because her opulent lingerie was becoming too tight. Had she been overeating? But she so rarely put on weight, she mused in bewilderment.

When had she last had a period? Tansy froze at that sudden thought and then opened her phone, where she had always kept a note of her cycle, only to discover that she hadn't even set up a record for the simple reason that she had not had a period since her marriage. *Not one single one!* Could it be that she was pregnant? The shock of that possibility thrilled through her and she thought of the pregnancy tests she had purchased some weeks earlier for just such an occasion, resolving to utilise one as soon as possible.

'Althea's been invited,' Jude informed her grimly, interrupting the frantic surge of her thoughts. 'Unfortunately, Isidore regards her as an old friend of mine. I should've told him what's been happening with her.'

'Just smile pleasantly at her and keep your distance,' Tansy advised.

'She's too brash to take the hint whereas you are probably the least pushy woman I've ever met,' Jude mused. 'I'm not sure that's always an advantage with me.'

'Well, I've never aspired to being perfect,' Tansy countered a shade tartly.

'And you're so prickly all of a sudden!' Jude complained, closing a hand over hers to walk her out of the bedroom, a tall, devastatingly handsome figure in an exquisitely tailored dinner jacket and narrow-cut trousers. 'You didn't used to be.'

Tansy reddened because she knew that she wasn't in the best of moods after the sleepless night she had endured, agonising over her feelings for him. 'There's a first time for everything.'

'I still like you, prickly or not, *moli mou*,'

Jude teased, closing a powerful arm round her narrow spine as they came to a halt in the door of the nursery.

Shaking off her bedding, Posy clawed her way upright in the cot, little eyes bright as she gripped the top rail and bounced in mad excitement. 'Da... Da!' she yelled, round little face wreathed in welcome.

'I still can't get over the fact that, although you say he didn't receive that money, Calvin hasn't been in touch to *demand* it,' Tansy admitted half under her breath as Jude cheerfully broke her rules to lift her sister out of the cot and cuddle her.

'She's supposed to be in bed to sleep for the night, Jude,' she scolded. 'That's unsettling for her. Routine is important—'

Jude dealt her an amused glance. 'It's equally important to be spontaneous sometimes as well,' he retorted in direct disagreement. 'As for Calvin, his number's blocked on your phone, which is why you haven't heard from him.'

'*Blocked?*' Tansy exclaimed in disbelief. 'How did that happen?'

'It was set up on your new phone before I

gave it to you,' Jude admitted without apology. 'I didn't want him harassing you.'

'You don't have the right to make that kind of decision on my behalf!' Tansy whispered in fierce dismay. 'Because he hasn't heard from me, he'll be even more furious and that's *not* a good idea with Calvin.'

'Allow me to deal with Hetherington,' Jude countered smoothly. 'He's my headache now. No way will I allow him to get his paws on this little girl again.'

Colour had burnished Tansy's face into animation and anger. 'That's not the point.'

'It's exactly the point,' Jude incised with cool, crushing finality as he settled the baby back in her cot and gently covered her up again. 'I am better equipped to deal with the Calvins of this world than you are.'

Having had access to the angry texts that Calvin Hetherington had already sent his stepdaughter, Jude was relieved that he had protected Tansy from them. So far, her stepfather had threatened to sell his story to the media and set the police on them for abducting his daughter without his permission. Tansy didn't need the stress of those threats. Jude was using every expert in the field to keep Posy's father at bay until another investigation by Calvin's former employers was complete. Regaining custody of the daughter he had never wanted was likely to be the last thing on Calvin's mind once he had more worrying developments to consider, Jude mused.

Jude's arm enclosed Tansy again on their passage down the sweeping staircase. Her colour was high, her mood on edge. Jude had a tendency to just take over, convinced that he knew better than her. But he should have told her about blocking her stepfather's calls, shouldn't have he? She would have panicked, she acknowledged, because she was horribly conscious that the law would be on Calvin's side as a birth parent and not on theirs.

As for Jude's words earlier... *I still like you.* It was better than nothing, she supposed unhappily. Not a lot to write home about though, when she was insanely in love with him! Perhaps she was a glutton for punishment, she conceded as they descended the stairs into a crush of the most unbelievably beautiful and glamorous women, who were all keen to personally congratulate the gorgeous heir to the

Alexandris fortune on his birthday. In short, Jude was being mobbed.

As Tansy stood off to one side, a waiter served her with a glass of champagne, and she asked him to bring her a sparkling water in a champagne glass instead.

Isidore Alexandris appeared in front of her. 'I believe Jude is taking you to meet his mother tomorrow—'

'Yes.' But Jude had mentioned that fact only in passing, and not for the first time she had received the impression that questions about his surviving parent were not a welcome source of conversation. Jude, she had sensed, was very protective of his mother.

Isidore compressed his lips. 'Stick by his side. Clio was difficult and Dion and I were hard on her because she did a lot of damage to Jude when he was a boy,' he breathed in a driven undertone. 'Her bitterness was like poison. Jude had been indoctrinated and traumatised by the time his father won custody of him. I still can't abide the woman but, to be fair, there were faults on both sides. None of us deserve a trophy for our behaviour back then.'

'Jude did refer to the...family bad feeling,'

Tansy selected with tact. 'But he doesn't discuss her with me.'

'He wouldn't,' Isidore commented wryly. 'He's very loyal to anyone he cares about, but I have never believed that she deserved that loyalty.'

As Tansy accompanied Isidore into the crowded ballroom, she saw Althea, glowing and gorgeous in a tight black dress that showcased her bountiful curves, and quickly looked away again. She was disconcerted when Althea approached her, dropping down fluidly into the vacant seat beside her. 'We didn't get to talk at the wedding,' the blonde declared. 'How are you finding married life?'

'It's wonderful,' Tansy responded with a smile to equal the brilliance of her companion's.

'Jude and I are incredibly close. I hope you don't intend to interfere with our friendship. Jude would be furious with you,' Althea informed her smoothly.

'I think that since you confronted him on our wedding day some things may have changed,' Tansy countered with quiet dignity. 'Jude wouldn't enjoy another scene—'

Althea's eyes flared with resentment. 'Who the hell do you think you are to tell me that?'

'His wife.' Tansy breathed in deep, studying the blonde, seeing what Jude probably did not see in his first love: a pampered and arrogant beauty unaccustomed to meeting with rejection. 'You had Jude once and you blew it. That's not on him, that's on *you*.'

As Althea spluttered in fury at that blunt rejoinder, Tansy eased upright in her high heels and walked away. A hand closed over hers and steered her behind an ornate pillar. She glanced up in consternation to see Jude gazing down at her with a dazzling smile of appreciation. 'I can't believe that I've reached the age of thirty before meeting a woman who wants to *rescue* me, *protect* me…'

'What on earth are you talking about?' Tansy asked, still flushed from her encounter with his ex-girlfriend.

'I overheard your conversation with Althea. You were warning her off for my benefit. That was very sweet,' Jude labelled softly. 'And very sexy.'

Relief that he wasn't offended, allied with that comment, made Tansy laugh. 'According to you, everything I do is sexy.'

Glittering dark golden eyes full of heat swept her animated face. 'It is,' he confirmed.

Tansy mock-punched his shoulder. 'You're full of it! Do some women actually believe that nonsense?'

'Unluckily for me, *not* my wife.'

Tansy stretched up on tiptoes and pressed her lips briefly, helplessly, against his. 'Give it up now,' she told him, wide green eyes locked to his compellingly beautiful face. 'You couldn't fake dejected, no matter how hard you tried!'

Jude pressed her back against the pillar and covered her parted lips hungrily, deeply with his and she trembled in response, every sense engaged in that intensely erotic connection. She could feel the fast beat of his heart, his arousal, the raw sexual tension in his lean, powerful frame and as always it thrilled her and only an awareness of their surroundings made her push jerkily against his shoulders to separate their bodies again.

Jude stared down at her. 'This is the first time you've been yourself with me today,' he told her, filling her with dismay with that unexpected insight.

'There's nothing wrong with me,' she protested weakly. 'You're imagining things.'

'I'm neither stupid nor blind, *moli mou*.'

Tansy set her teeth together. How on earth could Jude read her so well? How did he know that she was desperately trying to pull back from him to protect herself? Having realised that she was in love with him, Tansy had backed off. She would do the pregnancy test tomorrow, get that out of the way. If she *was* pregnant, it would take Jude's keen focus off her, wouldn't it? He would be delighted, and he would relax then and might well assume that any change in her was due to hormones.

All she had left now was her pride, she reasoned ruefully. The last thing she needed was to be humiliated by Jude starting to handle her with kid gloves in the same careful way that she saw him trying to handle Althea. Women who made the mistake of getting too keen on Jude might annoy and exasperate him but they also seemed to awaken his compassion. Perhaps that was a result of his recollection of his father's cruel treatment of his mother. But the very last thing Tansy wanted to be when they divorced, and remained in contact for him to see Posy and the child she hoped she was carrying, was an object of pity.

The giant tiered birthday cake was cut on the terrace beyond the ballroom where a firework display was staged simultaneously. After supper had been served, they were on the dance floor where Tansy was apologising because all she knew how to do during a slow dance was shuffle while Jude, of course, was as skilled on the floor as a formally trained dancer. In the midst of that, Isidore stood up and the music stopped abruptly as the older man called for attention.

Jude's hand, splayed to her spine, flexed and froze as Isidore addressed his guests with a beaming smile and called for Jude to join him at his table. As they moved forward, Isidore continued speaking in Greek and there was a loud round of clapping and many shouts of approval. Unaware of what was happening, Tansy stuck by Jude's side as he was slapped on the back and his hand was shaken by the many people approaching him. All she registered was that Jude appeared to be stunned but struggling to conceal that reality.

'Sorry, what's happening?' she whispered apologetically to Isidore.

'I've announced my retirement. Jude will now be taking over control of the Alexandris empire. It's time for me to step down,' his grandfather told her with satisfaction.

That announcement had made Jude even more the centre of attention. Tansy listened to him talk in Greek with apparent calm, but she remained conscious of the dazed light in his dark eyes that suggested that his grandfather's retirement had come as a complete surprise to him. She wanted to ask him why that was so, but Jude had been plunged into talking business with various guests and it was some time before they were finally free to head upstairs to bed and talk. It was two in the morning and Tansy was smothering a yawn, wondering if her bone deep exhaustion could be another sign of pregnancy, because usually she could take one late night without it being a problem.

'You're very tired,' Jude noted.

'Yes. Are you going to tell me why Isidore's announcement shocked you so much?'

'I had no idea that that was his plan. In fact, I thought he wouldn't even consider it until I was married with a child,' Jude admitted tautly.

Tansy stopped in the doorway of their bedroom and stared back at him. 'That's why you needed a wife and wanted a child,' she guessed.

'That possibility only added an inducement, but it's not why I needed a wife or chose to marry. Ever have the feeling that you've been played?' Jude breathed in a raw undertone as he doffed his tuxedo and poured himself a whiskey from the bar in the sitting room, kicking off his shoes, unbuttoning his shirt, the seething tension in his big, powerful frame blatant 'That's how I feel right now. Isidore *played* me—'

Tansy gave him a bemused look. 'I don't understand.'

'My mother, Clio, lives in an Alexandris property in Italy. She's lived there ever since the divorce. She got virtually no money when she left my father and Isidore allowed her to move into the Villa Bardani because initially she still had custody of me. He did offer to buy her a house in Greece, but she refused to come back here. A couple of centuries ago the gardens at the villa were a showpiece but over the years they were allowed to fall into ruin. After she lost custody of me, Clio became obsessed with restoring the villa's gardens. She had nothing else in her life to focus on.'

'Why did she lose custody of you?'

'She had a nervous breakdown and slashed her wrists when she was alone in the house with me,' Jude offered flatly. 'For that reason, she was deemed mentally unfit by the courts to look after a young child.'

Shock engulfed Tansy, for she had never dreamt that something so distressing lay behind Clio's loss of custody of Jude. His parents had had a dreadful marriage and it made Tansy wonder how much that truth had influenced Jude in his desire for a more practical union, shorn of emotion. After all, powerful emotions had proved destructive in his parents' marriage and must have damaged Jude's faith in them as well. How could he ever approve of love or even want it when some kind of love had originally brought his parents together? And Althea had claimed to love Jude as well, even after betraying his trust.

'Oh, my word…that's a horrible story,' she whispered in a pained tone of sympathy. 'Divorce, then a breakdown, followed by the loss of her son into the bargain. Your mother suffered.'

'Exactly,' Jude incised, his lean, strong face

grim and taut. 'This family *destroyed* Clio. I have a difficult relationship with her as well. She can't seem to separate me from my father inside her head. But I still care about her and believe that she deserves happiness. The gardens she restored over the past twenty years are now world-renowned and she's out there labouring in them from dawn to dusk with the gardeners. Those gardens mean everything to her…and Isidore threatened to send her an eviction notice.'

Tansy blinked rapidly. 'He…*what*?'

'She has never had a legal right to live there or even be on the property because it belongs to my family. My grandfather said he would throw her out and refuse her access to the gardens which belong to the villa unless I was married by my thirtieth birthday. I believed he would do it too, because he loathes her,' Jude admitted curtly.

'And that's why you needed a wife,' Tansy whispered, sinking down into the nearest seat before her wobbly legs could betray how much shock *she* was in. She had simply assumed that he had some business or inheritance reason for requiring a wife and it had not seemed worth her while to dig any deeper.

She had never dreamt that his motive might be so personal or so family-oriented. And that he had gone to such extremes to protect a woman whom he rarely even saw impressed her even more.

'Isidore was playing me,' Jude bit out harshly. 'He wanted to see me married and settled before he retired, but I suspect that he never had any serious intention of evicting Clio from her home.'

'Perhaps not.'

'Because it would have alienated me for ever,' Jude delivered with a bitter edge to his intonation. 'I assumed the worst of him, and he encouraged me to do so.'

Isidore had fooled him, Jude acknowledged, but, even worse, Isidore had *known* that his grandson would believe the very worst of him and that fact bothered Jude. Had he shown his distrust to his grandfather so clearly? Evidently he had and Jude's lack of faith would only have increased Isidore's resentment of his daughter-in-law. A tangled mixture of shame and guilt and resentment infiltrated Jude. Somewhere during the years of his childhood, he had discarded the ability to stand back and clearly read those closest to him. He had believed blindly in everything Clio told him, had judged his grandfather to be a cruel, hard man. Yet that same cruel, hard man had proved to be a loving grandparent, indeed a much more caring and supportive parental figure than Jude's distinctly distant father.

'Well, you may be married but I wouldn't say you're *settled* with a divorce already organised as a happy ending,' Tansy pointed out in consolation.

'I'm so comforted,' Jude bit out with a razor-edged smile, jolted more than he liked by that unwelcome reminder.

'I'm off to bed,' Tansy said, surrendering to the tense atmosphere, reminding herself that the perplexing rights and wrongs of Jude's family were not really any of her business because she wasn't a true wife. Not that Isidore appeared to appreciate that fact, she conceded ruefully. She saw that just as Jude had not realised his grandfather was wielding an empty threat as a weapon, Isidore had not realised that Jude might choose to make a *fake* marriage rather than a real one. Two tricky, too clever, too stubborn personalities from the same family, she acknowledged, well, fancy that. Jude and his grandfather were chips off the very same block.

Freshened up and sheathed in a silk nightie, she climbed into bed. Jude paced the sitting room, initially outraged that Isidore had duped him and unable to get past that fact. He had raced off like a knight in shining armour to come to his mother's rescue, but it hadn't been necessary. That was a galling footnote to the sacrifices he had made and yet hadn't Isidore created a better outcome for all of them? Clio was safe, Jude was, to all intents and purposes, happily married and newly conscious that he had a grandfather who appeared to love him.

Not a grandfather who viewed him solely as a necessary heir, but a man who had seen and possibly understood Jude's reluctance to risk his emotions in *any* close relationship. After all, emotions were messy and made you vulnerable, and Jude had perfectly grasped that fact after his mother, distraught over Dion's many infidelities, had tried to take her own life. Jude had been prepared to marry only if emotion could be removed from the equation.

And his marriage of convenience with

Tansy had scarcely proved a punishment, he reflected with a sudden grin at his own melodramatic frame of mind. Tansy was wonderfully straightforward, and hadn't he ultimately received everything that he had once craved? His freedom in business from Isidore's interference? The right to steer the Alexandris empire in a more innovative direction? It had taken the wife he had never thought to have to persuade him that his grandfather was not the callous monster Clio had once depicted. Jude had finally seen his grandfather's love for him as clear as day and it had shaken him almost as much as Isidore's retirement plans.

Naturally, his mother had had a confrontational relationship with his grandfather, who had remained loyal to his only son. There was more than one side to his parents' broken marriage and the divisions in his family were not as black and white as Jude had once believed. In a much better mood at having faced that truth, Jude went for a shower.

Gentle fingertips smoothed down Tansy's thigh, trailing against silk, piercing through her drowsiness. 'Jude,' she muttered.

'I'm sorry I was angry. It was nothing to do with you,' Jude husked, tugging her back against him.

'It's OK...' she mumbled, wriggling her bottom back into the heat of his arousal, registering the sizzle of awareness travelling through her whole body.

He kissed the nape of her neck, dallied there, found the slope of her shoulder and let his teeth graze the tender skin and a tiny moan was wrenched from her parted lips, eyes opening in the moonlight as she stretched back into the heat of him. His hands found the achingly sensitive peaks of her breasts and she flipped over and arched into him like a shameless hussy, finding his carnal mouth for herself. And all the inner tensions and insecurities she had been crushing down blew her wide open with hunger for him.

In one powerful stroke he drove into her and the excitement took over, pushing her into an electrifying climax that almost wiped her out into unconsciousness.

'That was absolutely incredible,' Jude husked, and that was the last thing she remembered until she shifted awake soon after dawn, dug out one of the pregnancy tests she had bought and crept off to the bathroom to use it.

Tansy stared in near disbelief at the positive result on the wand. She had had her suspicions, but she had not really believed until that moment that she *could* be pregnant. Her brain hadn't quite been prepared yet for that development and for a long time she sat on the edge of a glitzy bathtub, set in marble, contemplating the test. Her hand splayed across her stomach as she pictured a tiny version of her and Jude and her heart raced with happiness and a hundred expectations of the future.

Jude strolled into the bathroom naked as she emerged. 'You're up early—'

Tansy spun round to face him. 'I've got news!' she heard herself exclaim, excitement and a sense of achievement bubbling through her.

Jude switched on the shower and sent her a level glance. *'Yes?'* he pressed with subdued amusement, wondering what the heck she was so pleased about.

'I'm pregnant!' she told him.

And halfway into the shower, Jude froze, and he unmistakably paled as though she had given him bad news. 'Right... OK,' he breathed, vanishing into the shower, turning to face the wall, the tension in the muscles of his smooth golden back unhidden.

Tansy's excitement drained away like sand through an egg timer. She blinked, utterly at a loss as to why her announcement had proved to be a damp squib instead of a source of satisfaction and pleasure.

Jude wanted to punch the wall. The terms of the prenup they had both signed were etched in letters of fire inside his head. He had had every clause written according to how *he* wanted the marriage to play out. He had wanted his freedom back as soon as possible, had wanted a separation the minute he estimated it could reasonably be demanded. Back then everything had seemed so simple to him because he had assumed he would want his life back as it had been. But now, all of a sudden and without the smallest warning, he was discovering that what he had thought he had wanted wasn't actually what he wanted at all…in fact it was the very last thing he wanted.

CHAPTER TEN

WHAT WERE THE odds of a pregnancy occurring in so short a time? Jude asked himself, thinking of his grandfather, who had fathered only one child even though he had had three wives, and his own father, who had cast his sperm even more liberally and had *still* only managed to produce one child. And *he* got a conception in the space of a couple of months. Isidore would be jubilant, any kid, boy or girl, figuring as a virtual miracle in his eyes. In other circumstances, Jude might have been jubilant as well, especially if he could picture a baby like Posy, except with Tansy's hair and maybe Tansy's smile. Or a little boy. It wasn't as though he had any preference…

But for now he had to make the best of things, particularly because he had got what he had asked for, what he had bargained so hard to have. Where had his wits been?

Why had he not foreseen what might happen? What might go wrong?

Later that morning, Tansy toyed with the idea of saying several tart things to Jude once they were ensconced in the private jet and flying to Italy. But in the end she said nothing about the baby she was carrying, noting instead the frequency with which Jude's gaze rested on her stomach while realising that, in spite of his silence, he was hugely conscious of her pregnancy. And since that was the case, why did he have so little to say about it? In fact, it seemed as though her little announcement had utterly silenced him. Or was it that Jude was not looking forward to introducing her to his mother, who was, by all accounts, a challenging personality?

Tansy could only suppose that Jude was brooding because he now appreciated that everything he had done had been for nothing. He had gained a wife, a child in Posy and conceived another, radically altering his lifestyle for no good reason. In the end, after all, Isidore had handed his grandson everything he wanted on a golden plate. Yet, angry and hurt as Tansy was with Jude, she could not judge him harshly for striving to protect his mother. Conceding how hard she had worked to protect her little sister from harm, she had no right to judge anyone.

'How did your mother meet your father?' Tansy asked Jude abruptly.

'She was the gardener at a house he visited in Florence. He said it was love at first sight.'

'But from what you've said it was a love at first sight that only lasted about five minutes,' Tansy qualified ruefully.

'According to him, he told her before he married her that even though he loved her he could never be faithful.'

'When did he tell you that?'

'Shortly before he died when I was eighteen. I don't think Clio ever got over him. She still keeps a portrait of him in her cottage, which is a little strange if you consider the level of animosity there was between them.'

Tansy frowned. 'She lives in a cottage? I thought she lived in some big villa.'

'She *did* up until she lost custody of me. After that she moved into a house on the Bardani estate because she said she didn't want to owe the Alexandris family anything.'

'But presumably the cottage belongs to your family as well.'

Jude shrugged in dismissal of that point.

'I imagine developing a world-famous garden doesn't come cheap in execution or maintenance either,' Tansy murmured curiously. 'Who finances all that?'

'I cover her expenses, but the gardens are now open to the public and more or less pay for themselves.' Jude grimaced. 'The prenup she signed was so tight that she was left flat broke after the divorce. My father was needlessly punitive because she demanded a divorce that *he* didn't want and she had no family of her own to fall back on for support.'

'I can imagine that she didn't want to fall back on the sister who had slept with her husband,' Tansy said with distaste.

'Clio's still very much a loner.'

'What age were you when she had her breakdown?' Tansy pressed curiously.

'Six.'

'Did you find her after her…attempt?' Tansy asked tautly.

Jude nodded. 'The memory of it still haunts me. She was lying in a pool of blood, unconscious, and it was the staff's night off.'

'I'm so sorry,' Tansy breathed heavily as she attempted with an inner shudder to picture how such a scene would have affected a six-year-old. 'What did you do?'

'I phoned Isidore.'

'Not your father?'

'No, I knew he was partying in his yacht on the other side of the world because Clio had shown me the photos that day in a newspaper. I think even at that age I suspected that he wouldn't be much good in an emergency. Isidore sent help to the villa and then flew straight to Italy. He took care of everything and brought me back to Greece with him. It was two years before I saw Clio again because she was in a rehab unit for a long time and when I finally did, she and my father had a massive row, which just made everything worse. He had remarried by then and she couldn't cope with that. Their relationship was toxic long after the divorce.'

'I hope that when we part we can, at least, stay friends,' Tansy muttered tautly.

His brilliant dark golden eyes hardened and took on a glittering intensity that seared her. His lush black lashes swiftly screened his expression. 'I'm the last person likely to make the relationship difficult after the way I grew up,' he parried stonily. 'The children's security must come first.'

'I think you'll miss Posy when we split up,' Tansy forecast, feeling very brave in making that comment and admiring the steadiness of her own voice, but she felt the need to continually remind herself that their marriage was only temporary. 'I miss her now.'

Jude tensed and stared down at the laptop in front of him. 'It would have been selfish to make her do this journey with us when we'll only be at the villa one night—'

Tansy nodded agreement because she liked to try and keep her sister to a stable routine, which was difficult, she allowed ruefully, when Jude seemed to live flitting from property to property, country to country, and then there was the yacht to throw into his options as well. It was something they would have to discuss because there had to be one place he would surely be willing to call home where they could settle like a normal family. Only they weren't a *normal* family, she acknowledged with a sinking sensation in her tummy.

As they were driven from the airport it was a beautiful sunny day with the sky a clear cerulean blue and the landscape lush and green with the promise of spring moving into summer. Orange and olive groves and serrated lines of vines marched over the rolling hills and a colourful selection of wild flowers flourished on the verges of the lane they drove down.

'We'll head up to the villa later. Clio is expecting us,' Jude told her.

The limousine drew up at a picturesque old stone building embellished with glorious roses and greenery. 'It looks like a painting,' Tansy whispered admiringly.

'Wait until you see the gardens,' Jude advised. 'The whole place is like this—'

A tall, beautiful blonde appeared in the doorway and smiled widely at Jude. 'Come in…lunch is ready.'

'This is Tansy,' Jude murmured. 'Clio…'

Clio looked twenty years younger than Tansy knew her to be and she was still gorgeous, from her long blond hair and bright blue eyes to her leggy grace in workmanlike jeans.

'Tansy.' Clio extended a cool hand. 'Rather a common, ordinary herb, I'm afraid.'

Tansy went pink and smiled, ignoring the comment.

'There's nothing ordinary about Tansy.' Jude laughed, resting a hand against her taut spine.

A light lunch was served in the dining room. The room was dominated by a large portrait of a young, handsome man with black curls, his likeness to Jude so strong that it could only have been his father.

'The resemblance between father and son *is* striking,' Clio commented when she saw what had stolen Tansy's attention.

'It certainly is,' Tansy agreed, disconcerted by the older woman's brittle manner and tart tongue while marvelling that Jude was so tolerant of her idiosyncrasies. His kindness, his fondness for his only surviving parent were palpable, but it also helped her to understand why he would be so keen to steer clear of emotional entanglements in his own life after his experiences at his mother's and Althea's hands.

'Why aren't you drinking your wine?' the blonde woman asked abruptly. 'Don't you like it? Perhaps you'd prefer red or rosé? Or perhaps you don't drink?'

'Tansy's pregnant,' Jude said quietly.

The announcement dropped into a sudden sharp silence. His mother stared at him in dismay. 'You *can't* make me a granny! I'm far too young for that,' she objected vehemently.

'Fortunately, we don't need anyone's permission,' Jude countered quietly.

Clio settled indignant blue eyes on Tansy. 'Jude will ruin your life. He'll cheat on you like his father cheated on me. The last thing you should be doing is bringing a child into the chaos ahead of you!'

Tansy breathed in slow and deep to restrain her temper. 'You can't know your son very well if you think he would cheat on me. He has an aversion to infidelity that makes me feel safe on that score. He is *very* loyal,' she stressed defensively.

Jude closed a soothing hand over hers where it sat knotted into a fist of tension on her thigh. It infuriated Tansy that a mother could think so little of her own child that she denigrated him in front of an audience.

Clio snorted. 'You'll learn otherwise… eventually.'

Jude, evidently accustomed to his mother's attacks, made light conversation for what remained of the meal. Clio didn't even ask Tansy when her baby was due, indeed appeared to have no interest whatsoever in the topic. By the time coffee was served their hostess was becoming restless and she mentioned a media interview she had mid-afternoon before suggesting that they tour the gardens.

'Your mother's rather thorny,' Tansy said ruefully as they walked down an informal path from the cottage. The path gave way into a wide grassed area enclosed by a tunnel of low-hanging trees. An imposing stone temple sat as a focal point at the far end. It was spectacular.

'Always was. Essentially, if you had roots you would get much more attention from Clio,' Jude remarked wryly.

'No, I wouldn't, not with the connotations of a name as humble as mine. I think I'm the equivalent of a weed in her eyes!' Tansy opined with a helpless giggle.

'Thank you for not taking offence.' Jude sighed. 'She was rude but that's not unusual for her. She's not very fond of her own sex and she doesn't like to share my attention with anyone else.'

'Or the thought of being made a grand-mother.'

Jude flung back his curly dark head and laughed with appreciation. 'You weren't one bit bothered by her, were you?'

'No. You did warn me.'

'Years ago, she deeply offended Althea.'

'Althea has more of an opinion of herself than I do.' As they wandered below the trees, Tansy was relieved that she was wearing comfortable sandals and a light linen dress because, even in the shade, it was very warm. She was enjoying the fresh air and a sense of relaxation after spending half the day trapped in a seat.

'We have to talk,' Jude intoned tautly.

ESP fingered down Tansy's spine like spectral fingers of warning and her delicate features tensed. As her pace slowed Jude closed a hand over hers to urge her on. 'About what?' she said stiffly.

'I would suggest…a potential renegotiation of terms,' Jude murmured sibilantly.

'What terms?' Tansy almost whispered, so drawn tight were her nerves at that proposal.

'The legal terms of our marriage,' Jude specified.

Tansy tugged her fingers free at the edge of a mossy stone fountain ringed by wild pink orchids. Sunlight glinted on the clear water and the brightness made her blink several times. 'Why would we need to renegotiate anything?' she asked uneasily, her heart beating very, very fast in the heat, perspiration breaking out on her upper lip.

'You're pregnant. That changes everything,' Jude pointed out, lowering his lean, powerful body in a graceful sprawl of long limbs down onto the stone steps leading up to the temple. The fluid, careless elegance of the movement implied he had not a care in the world, Tansy thought painfully.

To Jude, Tansy looked very pale. But then that flawless porcelain skin of hers was very pale and translucent in comparison to his own, he conceded, studying her while willing her to respond as he wanted her to respond. In full sunlight, her dress was gossamer-sheer, outlining long shapely legs and the shadows of her areolae, accentuating the reality that she was not wearing a bra on her small pouting breasts. The tightening at his groin, the pulse of arousal made him grit his teeth, but she looked utterly incredible with her long streaky hair tousled in waves and catching the light across her shoulders, her clear green eyes fixed to him.

'I don't understand what you're getting at,' Tansy admitted shakily.

'In our marital agreement it states that the instant a conception occurs we can separate,' Jude recounted curtly. 'Of course, you're free to make your own decision and if that's what you *want*—'

'Separate…like *now*? Immediately?' Tansy prompted half under her breath, her lungs feeling deprived of sufficient oxygen in the hot, still air. 'Where did it say that? I don't remember reading that.'

'It was one of the clauses in the marriage contract.' She was looking at him as though he were talking in a foreign language, eyes wide, complexion white as milk below the sun.

Tansy was feeling impossibly dizzy and slightly sick and much too hot for comfort. She made a belated move back towards the shade beneath the trees, but it was too late. Darkness stole her vision, her body swaying, and she folded down on the grass in a heap as she fainted.

For a split second, Jude almost panicked. He raced down the steps to lift her up and she looked so white and delicate in his arms. He dug out his phone and rang the villa for a staff member to collect them in one of the buggies that were used by his mother's gardening team. Tansy stirred in his arms and moaned. 'I'm so hot.'

'You're going to be fine,' Jude said unevenly, trying to inject confidence into that optimistic assertion but very aware of his ignorance and digging out his phone again to organise a doctor's visit to check her out.

She was pregnant, rather fragile in his estimation and he had sprung a huge choice about the future on her without the smallest preamble. It wasn't only the heat that had got to her but probably the stress he had heaped on her as well and he felt appallingly guilty.

'You're holding me too tight,' Tansy whispered shakily, her head still woozy as she peered up at him, noticing that his stunning dark golden eyes were awash with emotions she couldn't interpret.

'Sorry,' Jude breathed tautly, his grip on her loosening a little.

'I'm still so dizzy.' She sighed apologetically as the world tilted and she was laid into some sort of compact vehicle.

'Close your eyes, relax,' Jude instructed.

But Tansy was incapable of relaxation with Jude's words still weighing heavily on her mind and shadowing everything: separation after conception. A clause in their premarital agreement? Why hadn't she read it properly? There had been pages and pages and she had given up ten pages in while the document went on to cover every possible and unlikely development under the sun. Even so, separating as soon as she fell pregnant? That was *so* cold-blooded, she reflected wretchedly. Had she been aware of that fact from the start, she wasn't sure she would have agreed to consider having a child with him.

Jude carried her up steps and she heard the low mutter of voices talking in fast, liquid Italian. Her head was still swimming but her lashes fluttered up and she saw a very grand landscape painting and she closed her eyes again, just relieved that they were indoors again and out of the heat.

He laid her down carefully on a mattress and she looked up into a crown from which elaborate brocade drapes were festooned.

Eyes widening, she sat up, ignoring Jude's advice to stay flat. 'Good heavens, this place is like a museum—'

'Isidore loves the villa's antique grandeur but he won't come here in case he runs into Clio,' Jude explained with a wry smile. 'It's not my style though.'

'You surprise me,' Tansy told him sharply, angry green eyes locking to his devastatingly handsome features. 'I would've thought the medieval vibe of magnificence would have appealed to you since your ideas seem to be equally barbaric.'

Jude stiffened, his dark eyes narrowing. 'I won't argue with you when you're in this condition and the doctor's about to arrive.'

'What condition? *Raging?* How dare you think for even one moment that it was appropriate to persuade me into a pregnancy when you planned to cut and run as soon as it happened? You think that's acceptable? I don't!' she snapped furiously. 'I don't need a doctor. I need a big stick or something to thump you with!'

Jude spread lean brown hands wide in an eloquent soothing gesture that had no effect at all on his irate wife. 'You're right.'

Tansy just glared at him, eyes as bright and luminous as jewels. 'You... *You!*' Words simply failed her and with difficulty she got a grip on herself again and twisted her head away sooner than look at him. 'I really don't want to talk to you right now. To have such a clause in the agreement you had drawn up...' she condemned. 'It was callous, selfish and unfeeling to ask me to have a child with you when you planned to walk out and leave me before it was even born.'

'I assumed that you would want your life and your freedom back as I believed I would want mine...but everything's changed since then,' Jude intoned, striding back towards the bed. 'Why aren't you listening to me?'

'Go away,' Tansy mumbled wearily, not in the mood to be placated when she was faced with the knowledge that she had been behaving once again as though their marriage were normal when it was not. How could she expect a level of support she was not entitled to receive? He had not told her a single lie about what their marriage would entail.

Of course, he hadn't planned to stay with her until the baby arrived! Why would he put himself through that boring duty of care when he didn't love her or plan to remain married to her? Jude was accustomed to doing what he liked when he liked. Great wealth had given him a freedom that less fortunate people could only dream about. She had been an idiot to make any kind of assumption about their convenient marriage, and what underlined that fact more than anything was a husband who talked blithely about *renegotiating* terms with her as if they were involved in a business deal.

'Tansy?'

'You can come back when the doctor arrives to translate,' Tansy told him grudgingly. 'Otherwise I don't think we have anything more to say to each other.'

As the door closed behind Jude, Tansy patted her flat stomach guiltily, tears burning her eyes as she thought of how much she would love her baby. She questioned if she would ever tell her child the truth of how she had ended up married to Jude Alexandris. Would she lie to conserve her pride? Pretend they had fallen in love? Jude being Jude would probably insist on telling only the truth. Her lower lip wobbled at the prospect of her son or daughter looking at her with less respect and more judgement. A business deal based on money. It sounded so sleazy and yet nothing with Jude felt sleazy. Why was that? Was she simply a pushover for his compelling appeal?

A doctor arrived, middle-aged and pleasant and with sufficient English to enable her to pretty much ignore Jude, which suited her mood perfectly. He told her that fainting was not that uncommon in early pregnancy, particularly when she had been tired and struggling to deal with the heat. She stole a glance at Jude, who looked as guilty as if he had pushed her down a flight of stairs and, instead of reassuring him that it had not been his fault, she hardened her heart and watched him leave with the doctor.

The salad she had requested arrived on a tray and she clambered off the bed and went for a shower before eating. She tugged on a light robe afterwards, reluctant to get dressed again.

When she emerged again, Jude was lounging up against the foot of the tall bed, looking ridiculously beautiful in his favourite ripped jeans and a T-shirt. 'You haven't eaten anything,' he pointed out.

'I wanted a shower first,' Tansy said stiffly,

averting her gaze from his riveting sensual allure. 'I shouldn't have shouted at you earlier. I shouldn't let my emotions go around you. After all, we made a business deal, not a marriage.'

Jude set his even white teeth together and flashed her a pained glance of reproach. 'That is not how I think of us being together. Our marriage is not a deal and it's got nothing to do with business.'

Tansy sat down at the table by the window and lifted her knife and fork. 'It is what it is,' she responded stonily. 'No point wrapping it up in euphemisms at this late stage. You *paid* me to marry you.'

'You married me to save Posy from an unhappy childhood. You didn't want the money for yourself. Obviously, that makes a difference.'

Tansy lifted a cool, doubting brow. 'Does it? You referred to renegotiating *terms*. That's business talk.'

'I was trying to be cool, clever. I shot myself in the foot,' Jude breathed in a driven undertone. 'I got it wrong. I get a lot of things wrong with you, but I don't really know how to tell you what I'm feeling right now…'

'Honest and simple works best for me,' Tansy told him, stabbing a fork into a piece of avocado, savouring its flavour while he studied her in growing frustration. She marvelled at the perfection of his lean bronzed features, the piercing intensity of his extraordinary eyes, and forgave herself for getting too attached to him. After all, she was only human.

Jude straightened his broad shoulders and rose to his full height. '*Thee mou...* I fell in love with you! I wasn't expecting it and I didn't immediately recognise it, so I messed up everything. I didn't even realise how I had changed until you began referring to us getting a divorce and it bothered me. I didn't want the clock to start ticking on a separation either.'

Her fork fell out of her nerveless hand with a clatter. 'You f-fell in *love* with me?' she stammered in disbelief.

'Understandably, I don't *want* a separation or a divorce now but there is no allowance for a change of heart in the terms of our marriage agreement. Nobody, least of all me, foresaw this development and, of course, it alters everything between us. I need you to give me the chance to prove that this can be a real marriage.'

Tansy had stopped breathing as well as eating. 'A real marriage,' she echoed weakly.

'I can see this has been a shock to you as well,' Jude commented, hunkering down beside her to settle dark golden eyes on her transfixed face. 'You'll need time to think about this.'

'Don't try and wriggle out of it again,' Tansy whispered with dancing eyes. 'You said you loved me... I want to hear the proof.'

'How do you prove something like that?' Jude groaned. 'The practical marriage I originally intended would exclude almost everything we have done together. I tell you everything. I've told you stuff I've never told another living soul. I feel very comfortable with you in every situation. You're very grounded, very calm and thoughtful. I appreciate that because I'm more volatile and impulsive. I think we are a very good match but whether we are or not doesn't matter because, at the end of the day, I don't want to go on living if I haven't got you beside me...'

Tansy dug her hands into his T-shirt and dragged him closer, almost knocking him off balance. 'Be warned. I won't *let* you live without me. I'm hopelessly in love with you but I'm terrified this is all some insane misunderstanding and any minute now I'm going to wake up and realise it was all just a dream!'

Jude's dark golden eyes blazed like molten metal as he vaulted upright and lifted her up out of her chair. 'It's not a dream. I was just a little too slow to recognise how I felt about you. There's been no special woman in my life since Althea and what I feel for you is much deeper than anything I *ever* felt for her.'

'Honestly?' she pressed as he brought her down on the bed and kissed her breathless.

'That was all first love, hurt pride and ego.'

'I still don't understand why Althea let you down in the first place,' Tansy admitted ruefully.

'We were each other's *first*,' Jude murmured. 'Even though we had no problems in that department, she was determined to try sex with someone else as a comparison.'

'Oh...' Tansy's green eyes had rounded in surprise at that information.

'*So...*' Jude purred, staring down at her with a new tenderness glowing in his beautiful eyes and a dazzling smile tilting his lips.

'You will have to content yourself to never ever having a comparison.'

'I'm very attached to what I got first time around,' Tansy confided as she struggled to extract him from his T-shirt. 'In fact, so keen am I that I just enjoy try, try, trying you again.'

Wicked amusement lit his amazing eyes. 'I love you so much,' he husked, claiming her parted lips again in a passionate kiss.

The robe fell open, exposing pale silky skin, and Jude took full advantage. Both salad and conversation were forgotten as the fever of desire took over and drew added fire from the depth of their new attachment. Passion and excitement combined until Tansy finally flopped back against the pillows and gazed at Jude with loving tenderness in her eyes.

'Why on earth did you talk about renegotiating terms when you *loved* me?' she demanded without comprehension.

'When you told me you were pregnant I panicked because I assumed that you would also be thinking of that clause in our prenup and you had already mentioned the prospect of us getting a divorce,' Jude reminded her. 'I honestly believed that you might already be planning to walk out on our marriage.'

'Idiot!' Tansy scolded, running gentle fingers along his strong stubbled jawline. 'You were the guy who warned me not to get too attached—'

'When I was already insanely attached to you…only I hadn't put a label on those feelings.' Jude flung his head back with a sigh, skimming narrowed dark golden eyes to her. 'It wasn't until you said this morning that you were pregnant that I realised why I was so happy with you.'

'And then you decided you needed to renegotiate.' Tansy grimaced.

'Not my most shining moment. But after getting to know Posy, I am incredibly excited about our baby,' he confided, warming that cold spot that his silence had inflicted earlier that day. 'I love her too…you know that, don't you?'

'There's a lot of love in the air right now.'

'But it was you who taught me to love again. Until I met you, I was so closed off from my emotions that I couldn't even see Isidore's affection for me,' he confided guiltily. 'I misinterpreted everything he did. I saw my mother's pain and blamed Isidore for it, but it wasn't his fault that my father was continually unfaithful to Clio, and I can understand that at the end of the day he chose to support his son, only he shouldn't have been so cruel about it.'

'She's your mother and she did suffer at their hands. Your father treated her badly and her experiences with him are still influencing her now. There's not much you can do about that.' Tansy sighed. 'But, thankfully, Isidore looks spry enough to be around for many years more and you still have the chance to show him that you care.'

'He really likes you. When he hears about the baby, you'll be the eighth wonder of the world!' Jude teased.

'I'm more worried about keeping Posy with us,' she admitted anxiously.

Cradling her tenderly in his arms, Jude gazed down at her with an air of satisfaction. 'I have good news on that front…although it's not good for your stepfather. I received a call about him late last night and another confirming his situation only an hour ago.'

Tansy stared at him. 'Calls from whom?'

'His former employers, my UK legal team.

Apparently, Hetherington was helping himself to money from clients' accounts at the legal firm. That's why they laid him off—they needed time to bring in a forensic accountant to investigate. They have concrete proof now and he's been charged with theft. He'll go to prison,' he forecast grimly.

Shaken by those facts, Tansy swallowed hard. 'Prison? My goodness, Calvin is not going to like that.'

'He was in a position of trust. That kind of crime is severely punished.'

Tansy nodded, shaken to think of Calvin in a prison cell and so grateful that her little sister had been safely removed from the fall-out of such a crisis.

'If he agrees to surrender his parental rights to Posy, I will offer him the services of the best criminal defence lawyer in the UK,' Jude told her. 'I think he'll go for it. After all, he's not interested in his daughter and doesn't want the responsibility for her. The lawyer won't be able to get him off the charges, but he may well be able to win him a shorter sentence.'

'Let's hope he accepts your offer,' Tansy murmured heavily. 'You know I never liked him, but I'm shocked that he was actually stealing.'

'I bet you made all sorts of allowances for him because your mother loved him. You have too much heart, but I'm not about to complain when you managed to fall in love with me even though I was behaving like a four-letter word of a guy.'

'I want to record that admission and use it against you in the future,' Tansy confided with eyes brimming with laughter as she laced her fingers in his ruffled black curls and drew him down to her again.

'You do realise that I'm never ever letting you go?'

'Cuts both ways,' Tansy warned cheerfully.

'How could I not love a woman who makes me this happy?' Jude purred, stretching against her, lithe and lazy, and pulling her close. 'You're my personal gift of sunshine and I love you.'

The same happiness swelled inside Tansy, assuaging all fear and insecurity. He loved her. He loved Posy and hadn't she seen that love in action? And he would love their baby as well. Contentment settled over her as she closed her arms round him, full of joy and love and possessiveness and no longer afraid of what tomorrow would bring.

EPILOGUE

FOUR YEARS LATER, Tansy sat on the beach on Rhodes, enjoying the sunshine while Posy and her little brother, Bay, built a sandcastle. Posy chattered incessantly, telling Bay what to do, groaning when his foot knocked a carefully built wall flying. Bay's mouth compressed and he loosed a shout of frustration, kneeling down and striving to rebuild what he had ruined.

'Let him have a go,' Tansy urged Posy before she could take over and do it for him.

'He can't do it,' Posy muttered in a long-suffering tone.

Tansy watched without surprise as her son carefully, clumsily patted the wall back into place. It was neither so neat nor so tall a wall as it had been, but it was a good effort for so young a child. He had phenomenal concentration for a toddler, and he preferred to build rather than destroy. Satisfied, he stepped back, watching Posy stick the plastic flag on top, and he beamed.

'Daddy see,' he said with decision.

Hearing voices, Tansy got up from the lounger she was on. She was slow because she was five months into her second pregnancy. Pulling on a beach dress, she heard the children yell, 'Pappi!' in excitement and race off to greet Isidore, who could always be depended on to visit with toys and treats.

Kerry, who had stayed in their employ, began shepherding the children back to the castle, but Bay was clinging like a leech to his father's leg, determined that Jude should first admire his castle.

The little boy looked very like his father, but he had Tansy's streaky light hair, though it was curly rather than wavy. Jude grinned at Tansy and performed the official sandcastle inspection for the kids, making acceptable noises of admiration. Isidore swept up Posy, who was chattering away to him.

Since Tansy and Jude had settled into a more permanent home in the UK, Isidore had become a frequent visitor. He loved to see his great-grandson and he did not make a difference between Bay and Posy, which had won over Tansy to his side. Jude had, however, had some difficult conversations with his grandfather about his mother and Isidore had acknowledged the part he had played in Clio's breakdown, admitting that his punitive approach and his unhesitating support of his son had gone too far.

He had made a magnificent cash gift to the Villa Bardani gardens in an act of contrition but Clio had had to be persuaded to accept it. Jude and Tansy visited Clio in Italy, but she had yet to visit them because she refused to leave her garden. While fences were gradually being mended and a new spirit of openness was growing in the family, they had yet to persuade Clio and Isidore to occupy the same room at a family gathering. Even so, Clio had made tentative moves towards being friendlier with Tansy, and the older woman was unreservedly fond of her grandson, Bay. These days Jude was a little more relaxed in his mother's company and she uttered fewer dire warnings about the likelihood of his continuing fidelity. Tansy was hoping that, for Clio, the past was finally staying in the past.

Her stepfather was still in prison. He had

received a heavy sentence for his crimes in spite of the excellent defence that his lawyer had made for him in court. That he had embezzled the funds of a disabled client had counted heavily against him. He had, however, surrendered his paternal rights over his daughter and, eighteen months after his court case, Jude and Tansy had become Posy's adoptive parents.

'We're dining on the yacht tonight, birthday girl,' Jude reminded Tansy. 'And you're all sunburned and covered in sand.'

It was her twenty-seventh birthday. Tansy lowered her lashes and then looked up at the husband she adored with gleaming green eyes of innocence. 'I suppose you'll have to harass me into the shower. Maybe you should have married a more decorative woman, who makes more effort.'

'But would she be as hot and willing in the shower with me?' Jude husked in her ear.

Tansy went red. 'Who can tell?'

'I can,' Jude purred, running a possessive hand down her slender spine as Isidore, the nanny and the children disappeared into the castle. 'I choose the sex bomb every time.'

'I don't look like one of those right now,' Tansy lamented. 'I'm all tummy—'

'That's my baby in there…that's wonderfully sexy,' Jude insisted, pausing on the path to crush her ripe pink mouth under his, tugging her up against his lean, powerful body and sending her temperature rocketing sky-high.

In the bedroom he presented her with an eternity ring. 'Eternity won't be long enough for me with you,' he swore.

Giggling helplessly at that high-flown assurance, Tansy headed for the bathroom, only to be scooped off her feet and taken there even quicker than her own feet could have carried her. Off came the beach wrap and the bikini beneath. Jude knelt at her feet, nuzzling against her swollen stomach while his deft and clever fingers made her writhe and gasp.

'We're heading out on a moonlight cruise, special dinner, all that jazz,' he told her thickly as she moaned at the zenith of her climax and went limp against him. 'I'm making you pay in advance in case you fall asleep early on me.'

'Took a nap this afternoon. I love you,' she whispered contentedly against his shoulder.

'And I adore you, Mrs Alexandris. You're the sun at the centre of my world,' Jude swore with passionate certainty.

* * * * *